Lock Down Publications and Ca$h Presents

I0658370

IMMA DIE BOUT MINE

Love Ain't Loyalty

By
Aryanna

First Edition 2023

Printed in the United States of America

This is a work of fiction. Names, characters, places, and incidents either are products of the author's imagination or are used fictitiously. Any similarity to actual events or locales or persons, living or dead, is entirely coincidental.

Lock Down Publications
P.O. Box 944
Stockbridge, GA 30281
www.lockdownpublications.com

Like our page on Facebook: Lock Down Publications
www.facebook.com/lockdownpublications.ldp

Stay Connected with Us!

Text **LOCKDOWN** to 22828 to stay up-to-date with new releases, sneak peaks, contests and more…

Like our page on Facebook:
Lock Down Publications

Join Lock Down Publications/The New Era Reading Group

Visit our website:
www.lockdownpublications.com

Follow us on Instagram:
Lock Down Publications

Email Us: We want to hear from you!

Dedication

This is dedicated to Tabitha Nicole with all my love.

Acknowledgements

I thank God and my family because both keep me grounded. I thank my fans and my LDP family for the motivation and loyalty. I thank my opps for the motivation because you all are funny as fuck! THE GAME IS OURS!

Chapter 1

As soon as I came out of the gas station and saw her, my steps faltered, and I damn near dropped the bottle of water in my hands. I couldn't see her face, but her thickness wasn't hiding in the slightest beneath her jean skirt. The way the sun shimmered off of her butter toffee skin tone made me wonder what she would taste like on my tongue. I was almost appalled at my thoughts and the way I was visually sexualizing this complete stranger. ALMOST! Wasn't it simply human nature and physics for a man to appreciate a woman's beauty first, unless he knew who she was? Being physically attracted to someone was what sparked conversations all over the world on a daily basis, so there was nothing wrong with my appreciation of the beauty before me, except for the fact that I was now staring at her like some wild stalker.

"Do you need some help?" I asked, moving toward her.

The sound of my voice pulled her attention away from the spare tire she had been trying to wrestle from the trunk of her silver Mercedes, and her eyes locked on mine. The sparkling green of hers made my mouth suddenly dry, causing me to immediately crack the seal on my water and take a nice sip. The fact that I recognized her now that I got a good look at her face damn near made me choke.

"David? David Bishop, is that you?"

"Wow, Tynesha, you gotta use my WHOLE government name out here in these streets?"

"Boy, please. Ain't nobody around or I would've had some help with this damn tire by now. I'm glad to see you though. It's been a long time."

"Almost three years since we graduated high school but you still look the same. Well, almost," I said.

"And what's that supposed to mean, negro?"

"You're beautiful," I blurted.

My response was simple, yet truthful, and caused her to blush hard in the afternoon sunlight. Tynesha Trotter had been one of the most popular girls in school, but she was down to Earth, and that made her beauty shine brighter. She'd had offers to represent the entire state of Florida in a beauty pageant, but she'd been too busy with school to worry about shit like that. Plus, she never took her looks too serious, which was hard to understand considering how truly gorgeous she was. Sometimes, looks like hers could make other girls jealous or insecure, but the truth was that most girls wanted the same thing that men did from her. Pussy! I hadn't personally tried my hand at convincing her to bless me with her physical essence though. I'd just admired her from afar and kept it as friends.

"So, why are you out here in the hot ass sun, trying to change your tire?"

"That's a LONG story, David, and I don't really feel like getting into it right now."

"Okay. I still wanna help you though."

I passed her my bottle of water before shooing her out of the way so that I could grab the spare tire and jack from the trunk. When I moved around to assess the flat tire on the rear driver side, I immediately saw what looked like a knife puncture mark, but I kept that observation to myself.

"So, did this model of Mercedes come with run flat tires, or did you have to invest in them?" I asked.

7

"They were actually my mom's idea. She worries about me being out on the highway by myself since I work at night."

"Good call. What type of work do you do?" I asked curiously.

"Boring security stuff but I'm a supervisor so it pays pretty decent for a single woman with no kids."

"So, you're single, huh?" I asked slyly.

I smiled at her when I asked this question, and I was rewarded with the same shade of blush heating up her cheeks as she fought a smile of her own.

"Yeah, I'm newly single. So, what have you been up to?"

The way she changed the subject was the opposite of subtle, and it made me laugh out loud, but I didn't press the issue.

"I do a little of this and a little of that. I'm a full-time personal trainer though," I replied.

"Personal trainer, huh?"

Maybe it was my imagination, but I thought I detected a note of disbelief in her tone. Still, I justified the decision to take my shirt off as me simply not wanting to get it dirty. I didn't have to look her in the eyes to know that she was admiring my 6'2", two hundred sixty-five-pound, muscular frame. The fact that she'd unscrewed the top on my water bottle and taken a healthy drink said it all. I quickly got to work, loosening the lug nuts on the flat tire, before jacking the car up in the air to change it.

"Still as handy as ever I see," she commented.

"I try to be."

"Well, since you're playing hero today, I'm gonna go inside the gas station and get you something sweet as a reward," she said.

It was on the tip of my tongue to make an inappropriate reply to what she'd just said, but I simply looked at her instead until she blushed and walked off. It was hard not to watch the sway of her hips and ass as she moved, but now that I knew who she was, I knew that I didn't have to be so thirsty. That wasn't cute to a woman of her caliber, and even at the tender age of twenty-one, I knew she was ALL woman. We were the same age, so I was going to have to act like it if I didn't want to get dismissed out of hand. I contemplated the approach I wanted to take when it came to asking her out while I changed her tire, but my thoughts were interrupted by the sounds of a car sliding to a screeching stop right behind hers.

"What you doing with this car, my nigga?"

The aggressiveness of the question got my attention more than the short, stocky dude getting out of the car asking it. The look in his eyes spelled trouble, but I was cool with that because trouble and I went WAY back.

"I'm changing the tire. What does it look like?" I asked sarcastically.

"That ain't your car, nigga. That's my bitch car, so you need to grab your shirt and move the fuck on."

I stood up slowly, but my mind was evaluating the situation at lightning speed. My eyes skated past the loudmouth nigga to the other nigga sitting in the passenger seat of the rundown Chevy, smirking, and back again. I could tell that the one addressing me had a pistol tucked into the waist of his shorts, but that didn't put fear in my heart. It was just another variable to the equation.

"Whose car did you say this was?" I asked calmly.

"My bitch, Tynesha. So, either you stole it or you know her, and you gonna have to explain either way."

"Roland!"

We both turned at the same time, no doubt due to the recognition of Tynesha's voice. The anger, hurt, and fear I saw contort her beautiful face made my heart beat faster, but I didn't move toward her like I wanted to because I knew that would only escalate the situation.

"Bitch, you got this nigga out here bout to die for playing Captain Save-a-Worthless-Hoe! Get your stupid ass in the car and get back to the house before I fuck some shit up out here!" He threatened menacingly.

Her glance in my direction was fleeting, but it was enough for me to read her mind.

"Listen, bruh, I don't want no smoke. I didn't know this was your lady, and I was simply trying to do the right thing. I'ma get out of you all's way though," I said, putting down the tools in my hand and picking my shirt up.

My comments seemed to fall on deaf ears because he never took his eyes off of Tynesha's slow approach. That was a mistake. As soon as I got close enough to him, I tossed my shirt over his face and punched him hard enough for it to sound off like a gunshot. His body bounced off his car, and I hit him again flush with a follow-up straight right hand. Before he fell, I grabbed the gun he'd had concealed. I could hear the car's door opening, but I quickly leveled the Springfield 1911 .45 at the passenger, halting his movements.

"Think about it because I won't hesitate to splatter your brains all over this car's shitty paint job while the street drinks your blood," I warned, smiling mischievously.

Dude put his hands straight up in the air before taking several steps back, turning, and running away.

"Tynesha, I want you to put the jack and stuff in your car and leave."

"But David, what are you…"

"I'll be right behind you. I'm not gonna kill this nigga in broad daylight. I'll meet you where we first met awhile back," I said cryptically.

I could see her hesitate for a moment out of my peripheral vision, but then, she quickly threw away the ice cream in her hands and followed my instructions. Once she pulled off, I snatched my shirt off of the barely conscious man and leaned down so that we could have an intimate discussion.

"Roland, is it? Okay, Roland, I want you to listen to me VERY carefully, as if your life depends on it. If you contact or speak to Tynesha again for any reason, I'm gonna cease your ability to breathe on your own. Now, you don't know, so you might think that I'm bullshitting. It's only gonna cost you your life to find out," I vowed.

I didn't know if he and any intention of making a comment, but I smacked him across the head with the pistol and rendered him unconscious. I used my shirt to wipe the prints off the gun as I headed back into the gas station, and I could tell by the expression on the cashier's face that he'd seen it all.

"If you feel the need to call the police, I'm sure that the camera footage will speak for itself. You can give them this too."

I set the gun on the counter and then walked back to my 2026, red BMW 8 series and got behind the wheel. I didn't drive away fast like I'd done something wrong, even though my heart was racing in my chest. I could taste the sweetness of adrenaline on my tongue, but outwardly, I was as nonchalant as always while my mind processed what had just happened. A day of cruising around Orlando and people watching had just turned into some shit straight out of my past. It had been awhile since I'd found myself in any type of situation like that, but some things you never forgot, and some skills never dulled despite lack of use. I didn't want to be that guy anymore, although I couldn't deny how ugly things might have gotten had I NOT been who I was. I put what had happened out of my mind as I navigated my car toward my old stomping grounds. I hadn't had a reason to come back to my old high school since I graduated, but it was the first location that I'd thought of for a rendezvous with Tynesha. When I pulled into the parking lot twenty minutes later, I was glad to see her sitting in her car, waiting for me. We both got out of our cars at the same time, and I could immediately sense the awkward tension building between us.

"Roland is my…"

"You don't need to explain, Tynesha. You don't owe me that. I just wanna make sure that you're good going forward."

"Honestly, I don't know. Roland is crazy, and he doesn't like to hear the word no."

For a moment, I saw a battered woman beneath the beauty, but just as quickly, she tucked that away and kept her expression neutral.

"Is there some place safe you can go?" I asked.

"Not really. I mean, I could go to my mom and sister, but I don't wanna put them in harm's way."

I understood her dilemma, and it kind of made me wish that I'd shot the nigga because that would've solved her problem. Since I didn't though, that left few options.

"Will you come home with me?" I asked.

"David, I can't…"

"I'm not suggesting that we share a bed or anything else besides a meal. You'll be safe though. I promise."

The range of emotions that swam through her eyes was hard to decipher, but the smile she gave me was beautiful.

"You're gonna protect me, David?"

"Absolutely."

"Well, then, I think I might like that," she replied mysteriously.

Chapter 2
June 2026

Common sense said that my eyes and mind should be alert for the police to appear and pull my Black ass over, but my eyes stayed on the rearview mirror to make sure that Tynesha was still following me. And my mind... my mind was wondering what my REAL motives were for inviting Tynesha to stay with me. True enough, it was my natural inclination to rescue a damsel in distress, and having somewhat of a history with the woman in question made it easier to give into that urge. It was equally true that visions of being in several compromising positions designed to give mutual sexual pleasure were rolling like film credits behind my eyes. I wasn't trying to come off as some dog ass nigga, who was nothing more than an opportunist though, so I'd been mentally checking myself during the whole ride to my condo. By the time we pulled into my building's underground garage and parked, I felt like I had my thirst under control. Barely.

"David, are you sure about this?" she asked once she'd stepped from her car and met me at mine.

"I'm positive that you could never be a burden or an uninvited guest. As long as you don't feel like I'm pressuring you in ANY way, you're welcome to stay as long as you want."

"I don't feel pressured. I'm extremely thankful to have such a good friend in you. It's just that… well, we haven't seen or spoken in YEARS, and now here I am, bringing my bullshit into your life and imposing. That's not fair, and I know that your girlfriend or wife will feel the same way."

"Tynesha, you're NOT imposing, and everybody has bullshit in their life from time to time. As for a wife or a girlfriend to feel some type of way, that's not something that you have to worry about because I have neither of those at the moment. It might take a little time for Stoney to get used to you, but that shouldn't be a problem."

"Who's Stoney?" she asked.

My response was a somewhat devious smile as I took her hand and led her to the elevator. It only took us a few minutes to arrive on the third floor, and as soon as I opened the door to my condo, she found out who Stoney was.

"Oh, my God, David, she's soooo gorgeous! Is she a pure-bred Pit Bull?"

"Yep, all red nose but she's a sweetheart so you don't need to be afraid of her," I replied, bending down to have my face licked in greeting.

Most people were standoffish when they met Stoney, just because they'd heard so many stories about Pit Bull attacks, but Tynesha immediately kneeled beside me and offered Stoney her hand to smell. Even more surprising than her actions was the fact that Stoney smelled her fingers one time and went straight to her.

"Wow. She does NOT take to anyone that quickly. Not even after she's seen them more than once. What type of voodoo did you put on my dog?"

"No black magic required, smart ass. Dogs are just naturally intuitive, and they have an uncanny ability to know the good people from the bad. So many people think that Pit Bulls are just aggressive, but truthfully, they are incredibly smart animals. Protective but smart."

I could hear the love she had for dogs in her voice, and it was sexy as hell. I quickly refocused my thoughts before I said something inappropriate, making sure to close and lock the door behind us before moving farther into my condo.

"Let me give you the tour real quick. As you can see, the floor plan is open, so that's the kitchen and dining room to your right and the living room to your left. Down the hallway, you'll find a bathroom behind the first door on your left and directly across from that is a spare bedroom. At the end of the hall is a loft, that I use for work when I do in-home training, and if you make a right, you'll find my bedroom at the end of the hallway. You can take the spare bedroom, the couch, or the loft, which ever you prefer. I've got a private bathroom in my room, so you won't have to worry about any privacy whatsoever. Look around, make yourself at home, and I'll get us something to drink."

"Thank you so much, David. It's really sweet of you to take me in like this. I can't put into words how much I appreciate you, but…"

"You don't have to thank me, Tynesha. I told you that I got you, and I meant that."

I'd meant for the smile I gave her following my words to be innocent and friendly, but the way she blushed told me that I might have been looking at her with hunger again. I quickly turned and made my way to the kitchen to find something to drink and pray that I had some food to offer her besides the can of cashews I kept for emergencies. My refrigerator revealed the bare necessities that I needed for survival as a bachelor, forcing me to pull out my phone and do an immediate Instacart food order from the nearest food supply chain. Thank God for technology's advancement and the art of ordering food around the clock. With that taken care of, I poured some food in Stoney's bowl and switched out her old water for some fresh water. Normally, the sound of these activities would bring her running into the kitchen where she would slide to a comical stop in front of her bowls, but Stoney was a no show so far. Instead of waiting on her, I grabbed two bottles of water from the fridge and went to investigate. I found Tynesha and Stoney on the floor in the living room, playing like two new best friends.

"I don't know if I should be jealous or happy," I commented, observing the scene.

"Well, there's no need to be jealous because you can easily get down here with us and play, and that will make you as happy and carefree as we are," she replied, rubbing Stoney's belly, much to her delight.

"Stoney loves me, but I feel like interrupting right now might not be in my best interest."

The way Stoney's head rolled in my direction made us both laugh because the look on my dog's face indicated that everyone had the right understanding. I chose to take a seat on the couch and assess what had happened in the last hour because none of it was what I'd envisioned for my Thursday afternoon.

"Are you hungry?" I asked.

"You cooking?"

"I'll save that surprise for another time, but right now, I was thinking about ordering a late lunch or early dinner," I replied.

"Late lunch sounds good, and I'm not really a picky eater, so I'll follow your lead."

"Okay, well, in that case, why don't we do something light like subs for now and let me take you to this great Cuban restaurant not far from here later? Not-not like a date... I mean, I just... You know like..."

"Relax, David. I know that you're not pushing up on me," she said, smiling brightly.

I could feel myself blushing under her teasing smile, but I managed to avoid eye contact while taking a steadying drink of water.

"You were always respectful and polite... and shy as shit too," she said.

"I was NOT shy, Tynesha. I just wasn't about to come at you or Tesha like every other nigga who'd never seen beautiful twin sisters before."

"That's the second time today you've called me beautiful. If you keep that up, then it might go to my head."

"Girl, please. You've ALWAYS known that you were beautiful, and a huge part of that beauty is because you never let it go to your head. I doubt you're about to start now."

"You're right for the most part. It's just nice to hear it from someone who is genuine and not trying to run game, so they can up the score with me as a notch on their belt. You've always been a real dude, David, which makes me wonder why we never kicked it on a different level back in school... Or afterwards."

"We were never single at the same time, and I'd never disrespect you by asking you to be my side anything. I can't lie though... I did wonder about you," I confessed.

"Oh, yeah? What did you wonder?"

The sensuality in her voice made the hair on the back of my neck stand up, and the way she was looking at me had other parts of my body willing to stand up and pledge allegiance. Before anything could come of the moment, Stoney picked that exact time to bark and scramble off of her back right before my doorbell chimed melodically.

"Are you expecting somebody?" she asked, raising a quizzical eyebrow at me.

"It's probably the groceries I ordered when we got here."

I followed Stoney to the door, checked the camera, and opened the door for the delivery boy. I passed him a $10 bill as a tip for his service since the food had already been paid for when I ordered it, and I took the two bags he handed me. I closed the door and turned to find Tynesha standing behind me with her hands out.

"I got it," I said.

I liked the way she ignored what I said and took a bag from my hand as she led the way to the kitchen, but I kept my comments in my mind to myself.

"Wow, you really weren't lying about not having a wife or girlfriend because NO female has been spending time over here with the way this fridge looks. Unless you just don't know that you gotta feed a bitch more than dick if you wanna keep her, even if it's GOOD dick."

"Very funny but maybe she ate all my food. You know how you women do once you get comfortable," I replied, chuckling.

"Oh, I can definitely eat, but your fridge looks like a burglary took place, and all they left was the baking soda."

I was laughing too hard to be embarrassed, but her teasing me did make me realize how few women I actually allowed into my personal space. I didn't do the casual smashing at my spot because it was almost impossible to shake a chick when she knew where you lived. Even when it was semiserious, I didn't do a lot of entertaining here because I didn't want an overnight toothbrush spot to turn into a drawer with her clothes in it that morphed into half of my closet space disappearing. The bottom line was that I liked my space, which made it even more weird that I'd offered my house as a sanctuary so readily. Questioning exactly why I did that didn't seem to be smart right now, so I just helped her put the food away.

"With all this food you bought, it'd be a waste of money to go out tonight, so why don't you let me cook for us? If you don't mind relinquishing control of your kitchen to me."

"Do you know how to cook?" I asked, smiling playfully.

"You think these curves maintain themselves? Besides, my mother would disown me AND my sister if we didn't know how to cook, so yes, I know how to throw down with the pots and pans."

"Alright, but I'ma tell you now that if it ain't everything you say it is, I'ma ride your ass and blast it all over Snapchat and Instagram," I warned, smiling.

"There may be some riding going on, but it damn sure won't be broadcast on social media."

I could feel my tongue sticking to the roof of my mouth and the air rushing up out of my throat like I'd been gut punched, but she didn't pause in the slightest when it came to putting the food away. The fact that she was smiling devilishly made it impossible to misunderstand what she'd said or what she meant, which left the ball in my court.

"Um, o-okay, I'm down to keep everything private - if we - if things go anywhere between us."

"Do I make you nervous, David?"

My immediate response was HELL NO, but the fact that she'd stopped right in front of me, and was no more than a breath away, made answering slightly harder.

"No, you don't make me nervous. I just don't wanna take advantage of you or the situation you're in right now," I replied honestly.

"What if I WANT you to take advantage of me?"

I didn't think that she could get any closer to me, but the small step she took forward brought us so close that the scent of her body wash was on my taste buds, dancing. Her eyes swirled with naughtiness and desire, but just beyond that, I could see vulnerability peeking through like a streak of lightening during a surprise summer thunderstorm. Knowing that this would be more than sex helped me to keep my raging desire in check and allowed me to take my time as I cupped her face in my hands gently. I watched her intently while slowly lowering my face to hers until our lips had their first introduction. The taste of her was indescribable, but it was delicious, and I immediately craved more. When she opened her mouth to me, my eyes lost focus, and all I could see was the bright light of her aura wrapping itself around both of us. The low growl in her throat that escaped when I grabbed her by her juicy ass cheeks, and lifted her o to the kitchen counter, had my heart hammering against my chest. I loved the feeling of her in my arms, and the intensity of our kisses was testing my patience. With her on the counter, my hand immediately shot beneath her Jean skirt, in between her thick thighs, and began pulling on her panties like they were offending me. With her assistance, we had them sliding down and off her legs in seconds, leaving only air and opportunity to finally bring us together.

I wasted no time dropping my shorts and boxers so that I could push my hard dick right up against her pussy lips. Instead of pushing inside her like I was aching to do, I stopped kissing her and pulled back so that I could look her directly in the eyes.

"Are you sure you wanna do this, Ty?"

For a second, her stare went completely blank, and it was clear that she was looking through me, in search of something elusive to me. When her eyes refocused, she smiled at me while reaching down in between us and taking ahold of my dick, pulling me inside of her warmth swiftly. Before I could settle in and get to work, Stoney started barking loudly from the other room. I could've ignored her doing this, because I'd done it before, but the fact that her barking was immediately followed by a deep, throaty growl from her got my attention. Sure enough, my doorbell chimed, and a forceful knock came with it.

"What are you doing?" she asked when I backed up and pulled my clothes up.

"Whoever that is, Stoney doesn't know them, and she doesn't trust them."

I could tell by the sudden fear on her face that she was thinking about the scene at the gas station, as was I. For that reason, I wanted to grab one of the guns I kept stashed around my place, but my instincts told me to check the camera first.

"Wait in my bedroom," I instructed, helping her down off the counter.

I waited until she disappeared around the corner before going to the door where I found Stoney crouched like she was ready to attack.

"Stoney, sit."

My command was obeyed instantly, and when I saw who was at the door, I was glad that I listened to my instincts. I opened the door and quickly stepped out.

"Can I help you, Officers?" I asked politely.

"Are you David Bishop?"

"I am. Why?"

"Hands behind your back. You're under arrest for assault and battery against Roland Simms."

Chapter 3

"Assault and battery? Did you even bother to check the tapes before wasting your time coming out here?" I asked, looking from one cop to the next.

"Yeah, we saw the footage, and you attacked Mr. Simms without provocation. Now, turn around and put your hands behind your fucking back."

I easily outweighed both of the white civil service officers standing before me, and I was taller, but they had that vibe that stated a willingness to fuck a nigga up. It had been a couple years since my last brush with the law, and I'd been lucky then to get away with unsupervised probation. From their approach though, it seemed like a safe bet that these cops were aware that I was good at giving out ass whoopings, and Roland wasn't my first nor would he be my last. Despite me feeling like this was complete bullshit, I knew that it could get worse if they searched my spot, and that was why I immediately stepped out into the hallway. I knew that their arrest warrant didn't cover my condo, but if they arrested me INSIDE my condo, then they could get around it. Reluctantly, I turned around, and the cuffs were quickly slapped on. While one cop read me my rights, the other one searched me so thoroughly that I felt like he should've bought me my dinner first.

"Let's secure him in the car before we toss his place."

"You can't search my house. Your warrant doesn't cover…"

My words were interrupted by my head's sudden collision with the wall beside my door.

"I don't recall anyone asking you shit, and if we DID ask your permission to search your residence, your answer would be yes," the cop standing directly behind me said.

Before I could utter any kind of smartass response, the door to my condo opened, and Tynesha stepped out with her phone in her hand.

"Good afternoon, Officer Michael Pinley and Officer Eric Leonard. It's good to see you again. Just so you know, this footage is being blasted all over Facebook Live right now, so I suggest that you make sure Mr. Bishop doesn't ACCIDENTALLY hit his head again like I just witnessed from the camera inside the condo. Now, are you here on official police business, or did my ex-boyfriend, Detective Roland Simms, send you here to harass us? Please think carefully before you answer that question."

The smile on Tynesha's face was a triumphant thing of beauty, even though I could tell that it was infused with A LOT of anger. She was calm, cool, and collected, but it was clear that she was with the shit if these cops wanted to push the issue.

"Mr. Simms swore out a warrant on this gentleman for assault and battery, and we're just here doing our job, ma'am."

The smile on Tynesha's face widened as she turned her phone around so that the camera was facing her.

"The excuse that you just heard from Officer Leonard's mouth sounds routine and plausible; however, it's bullshit. The man that you see in handcuffs is David Bishop, and he did nothing more than protect me from my abusive ex who was trying to force me to go with him. The same ex who did THIS to me."

When Tynesha pulled her shirt off of her shoulder, it was clear to see the fresh bruises in the shape of fingerprints, and that instantly had my blood hot. Now, I was REALLY wishing I would've shot that nigga, Roland.

"Officer Pinley and Officer Leonard, were you aware that Detective Roland Simms was beating me throughout the course of our relationship? Before you answer that, I should warn you that this question could come up again in a more formal setting, and the countless hours that you both spent at the house Roland and I shared will come into question too," she said, turning the phone back toward the cops.

There was no immediate verbal response, but I could've sworn that I heard one of these niggas stomach's rumbling like they suddenly had to shit.

"Ma'am, we're just doing our job and..."

The excuse was cut off by multiple phones ringing at the same time. One cop stepped away and quietly answered the call. I could tell by the soft chuckling coming from Tynesha that she had some idea of what the call was about, but I could only speculate at this point. Whoever it was didn't stay on the phone long, and the look on the cop's face changed dramatically once he hung up.

"Would you like to answer that question now, Officer Leonard, or do you have something else to say?" Tynesha asked sweetly.

Leonard didn't speak a word to her but instead whispered something in the ear of the cop still standing behind me holding onto my cuffed wrists.

I halfway expected the conversation to get heated, hut instead, Officer Pinley mumbled a few curse words under his breath while taking the handcuffs off of me and taking a quick step back. I turned to face them, ready for anything, but I didn't get so much as an explanation before they headed toward the elevator.

"Thanks for your time, Officers, and tell Detective Simms that I WILL be taking out a restraining order against him," Tynesha called after them.

Of course they didn't respond nor did they break stride. Tynesha quickly turned her phone back around to face herself.

"Now you ALL know who they're protecting and serving. Stay woke," she said.

After that statement, she hit a few buttons before putting her phone in her skirt pocket and looking at me. I could tell that she was unsure of what my reaction would be and that she was nervous as hell right now.

"Are you still down to order a couple subs?" I asked, smiling.

"You've gotta let me treat because I've put you through A LOT in the last couple of hours."

"Your money is no good here, but you can definitely tell me what the hell I've stepped into because it's obviously deeper than I thought," I said, taking her hand and leading her back inside.

I was somewhat surprised to find Stoney still sitting by the door, like I'd told her, but I was grateful that she was so obedient because her presence would've escalated the situation. With Stoney in tow, I led Tynesha to the couch and sat down. After ordering our food from Milio's, I turned to her and waited for her to organize the words she was preparing to speak.

"I met Roland about eighteen months ago at a club in Miami, and it was one of the biggest mistakes of my life. Shit was cool for the first six months, like most relationships, because people tend to hide their major flaws for a good minute. By the time the red flags came out, I was in too deep, and he'd made it clear that leaving wasn't an option. So, I stayed. I know that you're probably wondering why I stayed when I'm supposed to be this beautiful, strong, independent woman, right?"

"No, I'm not wondering that because I know that everyone in life battles with their own demons. I can't tell you how to battle yours nor can I tell you what demons to have. I can't judge you, and I'm not about to try," I replied genuinely.

The tears that suddenly appeared in her eyes made my heart beat wildly, but my grip on her hand stayed firm, and my eye contact didn't waiver. As badly as it hurt me to see her like this, I knew that I was here for all of it, and I wanted her to know that.

"The first time that Roland hit me, I convinced myself that I deserved it because I'd stayed out all night without calling. I'd been too drunk to drive, and he'd understood that part, but me not calling was unacceptable. I remember fearing that he was one of those abusive men on the low, but so much time passed between his first and second attacks that I forgot to be afraid. I mean, I'm mature for my age, and I didn't think I was naïve, but this thirty-year-old man had his hooks in me before I knew what hit me. His charm masked his manipulation, and that's why I didn't see all of this coming. Roland's abuse wasn't predictable, and I guess that kept me off balance for a while, but eventually, I got tired of it. It was either choose him or choose myself, and that's where I'm at right now. Leaving was the first step, but standing up to those crooked ass cops made me feel like my old self for the first time in a LONG time."

"How did you know that putting them on Facebook Live would have the desired affect?" I asked curiously.

"Because I knew that Roland would be stalking all of my social media platforms, especially since he had no idea where I'd disappeared to after you whooped his ass."

"Well, I appreciate the quick thinking on your part, but he most definitely knows where you are now. So, I think…"

"I understand you wanting me to leave, David, and I have no problem with that, but do you think I could take a quick shower first?"

"First of all, I wasn't about to suggest that you leave, only that you stay inside with the doors locked when I'm not here.

What type of nigga would I be to put you out in the street KNOWING that you've got a legal gang after you?"

"A smart one," she replied honestly.

"Well, then, I guess I'm dumber than I look because I'm not letting you go. You're more than welcome to take a shower though."

"How much time do we have before the food arrives?" she asked, stretching.

I checked the delivery app on my phone while trying not to notice the way she was slowly opening and closing her legs.

"Some time in the next twenty-seven minutes so if you wanna shower, I'll get you a towel and a washcloth. The bathroom is…"

"I know where the bathroom is. You gave me the tour already, remember? Now that I think about it though, I'd actually like to finish what we started in the kitchen," she said, suddenly straddling me.

"Are-Are you sure because we don't have to r-rush."

The hunger in her eyes was all the answer that I needed, but she was leaving no room for argument because her hand had already made quick work of my zipper. Before I could take a deep breath, I had the wind knocked out of me by her pulling my dick out and sliding down it purposefully until I was submerged inside her walls.

"Tight, huh?" she whispered while moving up and down slowly.

"Hell yeah."

"It's b-been a while so be gentle with m-me," she pleaded seductively, holding onto my shoulders for leverage in her mission of rise and fall.

With the way my dick was aching, it should've been ME asking HER to be gentle. It hadn't been that long since I'd had sex, but I couldn't EVER remember being in any pussy that was this good before.

27

My hands immediately pushed her skirt up so that I could grip her soft ass cheeks and pull her down on top of me harder. Her face contorted with beautiful pleasure whenever every inch of me was buried in her garden, making me want to give her more. She took dick the long way until her body demanded fulfillment in every way, and then, she started bouncing straight up and down on me. Within minutes, I was swimming in the deep waters of her ocean, loving it so much that I forgot not to join her as she galloped through the gates of Hell's peaceful death. We sat breathless, staring into each other's eyes with goofy grins on our faces as we waited for our hearts to slow down enough to talk.

"That was in-intense," she whispered.

"Yes the fuck it was. I wasn't... I wasn't ready for anything like that."

She blushed a deep crimson before lying her head on my shoulder and sighing in contentment.

"I always wondered if the dick was as good as they said or if you would prove too good to be true. Now I'm mad that I waited so long to find out."

"Shit, ME TOO!" I replied, laughing.

When she laughed, the vibration of her body made my dick jump, and before I knew what was happening, I was guiding her hips so that she was moving back and forth on my dick again.

The way that she bit my neck had me lifting up into her soaking wet goodness, loving the sounds of pleasure that were rattling her throat. The doorbell sounding off had the potential to fuck up our vibe once again, but she quickly solved that problem.

"Carry me with you and don't think about pulling out of me."

There was no part of me that was about to argue with her, but the trip from the couch to the door wasn't an easy one. Twice, I had to pin her up against a wall and deliver solid strokes that made her call out my name. By the time we actually made it to the door, the delivery lady was knocking impatiently. I opened the door wide enough to snatch the bag of food, but Tynesha slammed the door before any mention of a tip could be made.

"Finish me on the table," she demanded passionately.

Without hesitation, I pointed us in the direction of the dining room table where I laid her and our food side by side. This position allowed me to move her legs up from my waist to around my neck and gave me the ability to feed her punishing blows of love that forced her eyes to stare at her brain.

"Ohhh, David," she moaned.

"Ty-ty…"

The way I growled her name made Stoney bark at me but not even that broke my concentration. Her pussy was so wet and tight that I couldn't wait anymore, and I came with a hurricane's force inside her. Thankfully, my climax triggered hers, and we were able to ride the wave of delirious bliss together.

"I-I hope your microwave works," she panted.

My look of confusion made her smile.

"You're NOT just gonna fuck me like THAT and think we're done. It's my turn, my sweet David."

Chapter 4
One Week Later

"Where are you going?" Tynesha asked, grabbing my arm.

"To the bathroom, babe. I'll be right back."

The passionate kiss that she laid on me suggested that I hurry back to my bed because she was ready for me to put another hole in the wall with my headboard. In the past seven days, we hadn't left my bedroom unless it was absolutely necessary, and we hadn't left the house unless it was to walk Stoney. We HAD put two holes in my bedroom wall, marked each other's bodies with hickeys and bite marks, and discovered a level beyond insatiable when it came to sex. I considered myself claustrophobic when it came to monogamous relationships but being with Ty was different. I couldn't get enough of her, and the fact that she felt the same way had made the last week vanish like a magic trick. I'd never spent this much uninterrupted time with any one woman, and the thought of it had always made me itch, but whatever was happening between us felt RIGHT. I didn't want to say anything because I feared that words might fuck it up or complicate it. It was obvious that she was feeling me though and not in no REBOUND kind of way. She had me wondering how far things could really go between us. After I pissed and washed my hands, I made my way back to my room with the intentions of slick like bringing up our possibilities in a casual way, but I found her sitting up in bed on her phone. The sight of her naked body caused a familiar tingle to shoot through me, pushing all thoughts of talking from my mind. Before I could climb back in the bed though, I picked up on her vibe, and that made me study her face a little closer. She wasn't talking, but whoever or whatever she was listening to had her undivided attention.

"Everything okay?" I whispered.

She gave me a quick nod before pushing a button on her phone and listening some more. Once she had another earful, she hung up the phone and looked at me in a weird way.

"I'm pretty sure that this ain't the first time you've seen me naked this week, so why are you staring?" I asked curiously.

"I just got a message from my mom, and she's insisting that I climb off the dick and bring you to dinner tonight."

"When did you tell your mom about us?" I asked.

I was hoping that the sudden panic I could feel in my throat hadn't come out with my question but going public with the parents was a BIG DEAL. It wasn't a step that I'd ever taken before, and it damn sure wasn't on my current bucket list.

"I didn't tell my mom anything about us, which means that information could've only come from Tesha's big mouth ass."

I hadn't interacted with Tesha as much as I had Tynesha in high school, but I knew enough to know that they had more differences than similarities. They were identical twins, but Tesha was more brazen, and her personality was more in your face. Tynesha was the type to resolve conflicts in private, if possible, whereas Tesha had beat a bitch from one side of the cafeteria to the other just for sport.

Hearing that she hadn't kept her sister's secret didn't surprise me, but I had a feeling it was about to affect me.

"So, what exactly did you tell your sister about us?"

The guilty smile that instantly lit up her face said a lot, but the way her eyes scanned my nakedness from head to toe said it all.

"Ah, so you kissed and told, huh?" I teased.

"David, I would never do… okay, maybe I told a LITTLE BIT."

All I could do was laugh as I slid back onto the bed beside her and leaned up against the headboard.

"So, what are you about to call your mom and say?"

"That depends on how you feel about going to dinner. I mean, I know that whatever is happening between us was completely unexpected, but I hope you know that it's not just sex for me. I would like for us to have a future, David, but I can't want that for both of us."

The vulnerability of her words and the look in her eyes made me pull her toward me without hesitation. There was no denying how unexpected all of this had been, and still was, but it still felt amazing and effortless. I liked being with Tynesha because I didn't have to be anyone other than myself. When it came to most women, I had to hide my 'bad boy' ways, especially when it came to being in the streets or womanizing. I didn't have to do that with Ty because she knew who I used to be, she accepted it, and she understood that I'd grown from it. Plus, she was an amazing woman, so only a crazy man wouldn't want to be with her. After getting to know her in the most intimate of ways, I better understood what had driven Roland to madness too because the pussy was TORCH!

"I'm down to share a meal with you and your people, but I'ma need you to tell me what I'm walking into."

"Honestly, David, I have NO idea. I ain't never took a nigga home to meet my family, especially not for something as serious as a meal. Roland wouldn't do no shit like that, and I doubt I would've asked anyway."

Part of me felt flattered that I was getting ready to break new ground but not having a blueprint to follow meant that

I couldn't prepare for the unseen obstacles that surely awaited. Was the feeling in my chest anxiety? That was as foreign to me as having a live-in girlfriend, but I'd never been one to bow to the weaknesses that I recognized in myself.

"Well, if we're doing this then we better take a shower first," I suggested.

The smile that she gave me when she looked up at me was a mixture of gratitude and relief, but when she leaned up off of me, I saw the naughty twinkle in her eyes.

"We can take a shower if you want, but you're still gonna smell like this good pussy."

I wasn't sure what that meant exactly. I simply took her offered hand and followed her to the bathroom. I thought that we would've made more steam than the hot water all around us, but we only bathed each other sensually and then got out of the shower. It wasn't until I was fully dressed that I found out what her comment meant.

"What are you doing?" I asked when she pushed me down on the bed.

"You'll see."

She quickly straddled me, pushing her jean skirt up over her hips as she pulled my dick out of my shorts. Within seconds, I was deep inside her pussy, loving the way she dripped all over me as she rode me fast and hard. I tried grabbing her hips to control her speed, but she put my hands on her titties and made me squeeze while she worked me. I didn't even get the chance to beg because in under two minutes, she made me cum until I was weaker than a newborn kitten. All I could do was lie there when she climbed off me. I watched in utter fascination as she calmly pulled on one of my t-shirts and knotted it at her waist before putting her panties on.

"Remind me to get some clothes while we're at my mom's house since we haven't found time to go to my spot," she said.

I could only grunt a response while I waited on coherent thoughts to return to my orgasm fried brain cells. Her soft laughter probably should've made me feel embarrassed somewhat, but it didn't in the slightest.

"Let me help you out, baby," she said, leaning over me.

The feeling of her soft hands on my dick caused me to moan involuntarily, but when she suddenly took me into her mouth, I stopped breathing altogether. I watched as she rhythmically bobbed at a slow pace, up and down, staring at me hungrily while my dick disappeared down her throat again and again. Within moments, her lips and throat had worked like jumper cables, and I was back to spectacular rock-hard form.

"Wh-what are you doing?" I asked when she suddenly stopped and got up.

"We've gotta go, bae. I'll finish you off later."

Every fiber of my being wanted to argue, and gently grab a handful of her hair so she wouldn't move, especially because she had yet to finish me off with her mouth EVER. I didn't say shit though. I just tucked my dick back into my shorts and got up.

"Awww, baby, don't be upset. It was your idea that we leave the house, but I promise that, as soon as we get back, I'll go back to being your willing sex slave," she vowed seductively.

The kiss she gave me following this promise made my frustration dissipate immediately. There was no denying it; I was whopped already. I waited patiently for her to finish getting ready, and once I made sure Stoney was straight for a few hours, we left.

"I'll drive," she said, taking my keys from my hand and going to my driver's side door.

I paused briefly because my initial response was to tell her that I didn't let ANYBODY drive my car, but the reality was that she wasn't just anybody. Ty was definitely different and important to me, so I got my happy ass in the passenger seat and kept my mouth shut. She whipped my car like she'd been driving it for years, but the fact that before she'd pulled out of the lot, she took my hand in hers kept me quiet and content. We cruised through Orlando as afternoon gave way to evening, pulling up at the house that her mom and sister shared a half an hour later.

"You ready?" she asked, looking over at me.

"As ready as you are, I guess."

"You'll be fine. Don't worry. You already know Tesha's loudmouth ass, and now you're about to see where she gets it from. I take after my dad, whoever that nigga is."

"I think I'd be more afraid to meet him, especially smelling like what we just did," I said, smiling ruefully.

"Yeah, I bet."

We got out of the car and headed up the sidewalk to the front door of the split-level house. I spotted a curtain moving in a room upstairs, but I didn't see who was peeping out from behind it. We made it to the porch, but before Ty could knock on the door, it was pulled open, and a slightly older, equally beautiful, version of her stepped out. Tynesha and Tesha's mom had a honey gold skin tone with only a few wrinkles around her green eyes to give away the fact that she wasn't a teenager herself. The white catsuit hugging her curves looked like it was chiseled marble, and it was clear she had some thickness behind her. The twins might not know who their dad was, but it was obvious who they inherited their beauty from.

"So, this is who had you missing for a week? You're cute, but the next time you kidnap my daughter, you're gonna have to answer to me."

"Yes, ma'am," I replied contritely.

"My name is Tonya, and if you call me ma'am again, you won't be welcome in my house. Understood?"

"Yes, m… Yes, Tonya."

The fact that Tynesha was giggling wasn't helping my nerves any, but I completely froze up when her mom came toward me with open arms. It would've been impolite not to hug her, so I did, but I was praying it didn't last too long.

"I like the cologne you're wearing, David. It's the scent of good pussy, right?" Tonya asked casually.

Tynesha's giggles turned to loud cackles, but my mouth fell open in shock. Thankfully, her mom didn't keep me on the spot for that long and instead moved to hug her daughter before leading us inside. When Tynesha's hand slipped back into mine, I squeezed it purposefully and gave her a look that let her know she OWED ME. Her wink and the thorough licking of her lips signaled her understanding, but that only made me feel slightly better because I knew I still had to endure the hot seat in order to get to the promise land.

"What's for dinner, Mom?" Tynesha asked once we'd made it to the kitchen.

"Ham, macaroni and cheese, collard greens, cornbread, and baked beans. I need you to tell your sister to run to the store and grab a bottle of red wine because we're out. You can change your clothes while she's doing that because if I'm not mistaken, you had that same skirt on when you last Snapchatted me."

"I ain't had to wear clothes all week, but you're right. I do need to change," Tynesha said, smiling.

Before I could shoot her a look telling her not to leave me alone, she'd let go of my hand and disappeared back up the hallway.

"You can take a seat, David. I don't bite... at least not hard."

The smile on Tonya's face was more predatory than anything I'd ever seen on Animal Planet, but I took a seat at the kitchen table anyway.

"So, I caught Tynesha's Facebook Live post last week. Did you really step in and help my daughter?"

"Yeah. Dude showed up at the gas station while I was changing her tire, and I could tell by the look on Ty's face that she didn't wanna go with him. So, I did what I had to do," I replied nonchalantly.

"I appreciate that, David. That was definitely some real nigga shit you did. Hopefully, Roland backs off for good, or somebody MAKES him back off."

There was no way to misinterpret what Tonya was saying, and I'd had the same thoughts enough times over the last week to agree with what she was thinking. I didn't verbally respond, but I nodded my head in understanding.

"Ordinarily, I'd probably grill the shit out of you because I love my daughters very much, but I believe I know the kind of man you are, so I'll spare you. I am gonna need you to go upstairs to the bathroom at the top of the steps and wash your dick before you eat dinner with us."

"Yes, ma'am," I replied, completely embarrassed.

"I told you outside about that yes ma'am shit, David, so consider this your last warning."

I nodded before quickly making my way from the room and heading for the stairs we'd walked past when we came in. I would do what Tonya asked, but first, I was going to have a word with Tynesha. Thankfully, I didn't have to look for her because she was headed to the bathroom.

"Oh, NOW you wanna take a shower! We could've done that at my house instead of you insisting that we come here smelling freshly fucked. WHY did you do that anyway? Were you marking your territory or something because you HAD to know that your mom was gonna speak on us smelling like sex?" I said, slightly frustrated.

Her response was to laugh while pulling me into the bathroom with her. She closed the door behind us and immediately pulled of the towel she was wearing to reveal her nakedness. It was a battle to keep my eyes locked on her face, but I refused to be distracted by the prospect of sex.

"Tynesha, this shit is too crazy! I came here intending to make a good impression on your mom and sister, but now, I… I… Oh, shhhhiittt," I moaned.

While I'd been talking, she'd dropped to her knees and now had my dick in her mouth like her favorite pacifier. I was fighting not to give in to her, but all of my defiance evaporated when she put both of my hands on her head and went to WORK on the dick. I could feel my toes curling through my shoes, forcing me to pull her hair in a way that I knew would cause her pain. She didn't stop though nor did she slow down or lose her rhythm. She wasn't sucking my dick. She was determined to drain the life force from it.

"You... You're gonna make me cum," I whispered fiercely.

I thought that hearing this might've slowed her down, but she increased in both speed and pressure. With the stealth of the Grim Reaper, my climax appeared, and suddenly, I was cumming intensely enough to make my knees knock. Watching her catch and swallow every drop of my protein only made the experience more erotic. Just when I thought it couldn't get any better, she pulled my dick out of her mouth and rubbed it all over her face to smear the last droplets of cum on her flawless skin. I watched in awe as she smiled at me while rubbing it into her skin like it was Olay moisturizing cream.

"You shouldn't look so surprised, David. Everybody knows that cum is good for the skin."

My surprise quickly turned to shock as the sound of her voice penetrated the fog around my brain.

"Oh, shit," I said slowly.

"Shhh, it's okay, David. This will forever be our little secret because I promise you that I won't tell Tynesha what just went down."

Chapter 5

"David? Baby, did you hear me? I asked what you want to eat on your plate."

"You... You can put everything on there," I replied, smiling at Tynesha while trying to ignore the smirk on Tesha's face.

Here I was, still trying to wrap my mind around what the fuck just happened twenty minutes ago upstairs, but Tesha was clearly unfazed by it. I'd spent long moments splashing cold water on my face from the bathroom sink, trying to erase the shock of Tesha sucking my dick, and she'd calmly hopped in the shower. The crazy bitch even had the nerve to sing like it was a completely ordinary day, and her song choice of Mary J. Blige's hit, *I'm Going Down*, didn't help my mood. I was anything but calm because I hadn't been able to figure out if the shakiness I felt was due to fear of Tynesha finding out what had happened or my body's excitement from what had happened. Now that we were all seated around the table, and my secret was still safe, I could admit that the feeling in my body then and now was excitement from what had happened. I was feeling Tynesha for sure, but her sister sucked dick like a porn star, and that shit was SEXY!

"So, David, what have you been up to since high school?" Tesha asked politely.

"Um, not much really. I do odd jobs to earn extra cash, but I'm a personal trainer full time."

"I can tell that you bulked up a little since the last time I saw you, but your size is perfect," Tesha replied, smiling mischievously.

Thankfully, Tonya came back into the room, set the plate and cornbread on the table, and took her seat because I felt like the conversation was about to go left.

"So, um, what have you been up to, Tesha?" I asked.

"I do a little modeling here and there, mainly for online clothing and lingerie. My ass looks AMAZING in a pair of jeans... or some cute little boy shorts. Lately, I've been thinking about enrolling in college though."

"You didn't mention that to me," Tynesha said, coming back into the dining room and sitting my plate in front of me.

"Well, you've been too preoccupied with your new boo thang to answer my calls, bitch, but I see why," Tesha said, laughing.

I tried to avoid eye contact with anyone because I felt like Tynesha and her mom could simply look at us and know that some shit had went down, but I still caught a glimpse of something naughty in Tesha's expression.

"Well, I'm glad that you THINK you understand, but either way if you would've hit me up on some important shit like you going back to school, I would've made time for you. David would've understood, plus I'll never be too busy for you and Mom," Tynesha replied genuinely.

"Awww, baby, that's sweet, but I suggest that you never take good dick for granted," Tonya said.

The three of them shared a laugh, but I wisely kept my mouth shut tight. Whatever comment I could make would only serve as quicksand, and my Black ass wasn't trying to go down like that.

"So, what are you thinking about studying?" I asked, hoping to refocus the topic away from my lower anatomy.

"I'm not sure yet, but I'm leaning towards criminal justice. I respect the strides that have been made with regards to trying to reverse mass incarceration for minorities, but there's still a LONG WAY to go in that fight."

"Amen," Tynesha said, nodding her head.

I hid my surprise by picking up my fork and tasting the food in front of me. Out of the two of them, Tynesha had always struck me as the more socially conscious, book smart sister, but apparently, there were things about Tesha that I didn't know. The look that she was giving me indicated that she didn't mind teaching me a thing or two either.

"When was the last time you had some home cooking like this?" Tynesha asked, smiling at me.

"I can't even remember. Tonya, you did your thing," I replied hungrily around a mouthful of macaroni and cheese.

"Thank you, baby. I try to do what I can. My cooking seems to be the only thing that gets Tynesha to come home anymore."

"I'm sorry that I haven't been around, Mom. I didn't wanna involve you and Tesha in my bullshit and drama, so it seemed like the best solution was to stay away."

"Yeah, well, don't EVER do no shit like that again. I raised both of you girls to be strong, independent, Black women, and you better not ever let a muthafucka control you or abuse you."

"Amen." Tesha chimed in.

"She ain't gotta worry about that no more," I stated quickly.

The look I turned on Tynesha made her blush beautifully, and I suddenly felt her hand on my thigh. I didn't jump when she touched me, but it was a battle not to do just that when I felt Tesha's foot making its way up my leg. Tynesha was sitting to my right, and her mom was to my left, so there was no doubt that the foot rubbing up and down my leg slowly belonged to Tesha. I glanced at her briefly before going back to my food, but she and her eyes fixed on her own food as if that was all she cared about.

"So, what are your intentions with my daughter, David?"

"Really, Mom?" Tynesha asked, embarrassed.

"If this conversation makes you feel uncomfortable, sweetie, you can make yourself busy by bringing out the wine you got from the store," Tonya said.

"Just BE NICE," Tynesha replied.

The reassuring squeeze that she gave my thigh before getting up from the table didn't exactly make me feel better, but I didn't let it show. As long as Tonya was in the room, I didn't feel like I had anything to fear. The mention of the wine did send my mind back to what happened upstairs though, causing me to shake my head to clear my mind. I felt like a lame because I was combatting the guilt creeping around my heart with the justification that if Tynesha had told me that SHE was going to the store instead of Tesha, IT wouldn't have happened. Right now, the truth didn't taste as good as the food in front of me, and it was too much to swallow.

"My intentions with tour daughter? Well, I intend to be the good man that I am and let that speak for itself. I could feed you a bunch of pretty words, but my actions are the only things that matter," I stated honestly.

"One thing that I remember about you, David, is that you're DEFINITELY a man of action," Tesha said, smiling brightly.

"I bet," Tonya said, chuckling softly.

I expected more questions or for either woman to press the issue, but we all settled into a comfortable silence while enjoying the food.

"Why is everyone so quiet? What did you say, Mom?" Tynesha asked, coming back into the room with the wine in her hand.

"I didn't say nothing, baby. David seems like a good guy, so he deserves to be given the benefit of the doubt and not immediate distrust."

I could tell by the look on Tynesha's face that Tonya's simple explanation caught her by surprise and made her suspicious. She let it go though, pouring me and her a glass of wine before passing the bottle to her mom. We spent the remainder of the meal laughing and talking like this was a normal nightly gathering for us, and eventually, I was able to momentarily forget that I should've felt like a piece of shit for cheating on Ty with her twin. Once the food and wine were gone, Ty gave me a look that said I needed to get her back behind closed doors and feed her dessert.

"Tonya, I appreciate the meal, but if I don't get out of this chair and get home, I'ma be sleeping right where I am," I said.

"I'll get you a blanket if you want, but we've got plenty of beds in this house," Tesha offered teasingly.

"Nah, we're gonna head out," Tynesha said, grabbing my hand and standing up.

I followed her lead, already envisioning her soft skin under my fingertips and the taste of her body on my tongue.

"Alright, well, you two get home safe, and David, don't kidnap my daughter again for seven days. Don't choke her with the dick. Make sure she comes up for air."

"And don't smother him either, sis. Let my boy breathe," Tesha said, smiling at me.

"Thanks for the advice, you two, and good night."

With that said, Tynesha quickly pulled me out of the house and maneuvered me to the driver's side door of my car.

"You're driving because I've had too much to drink, and I can only focus on one thing at the moment."

"And what's that?" I asked knowingly.

"How fucking HORNY I am!"

Her words made my dick hard, and her smile had my tongue stuck to the roof of my mouth. I didn't waste a moment getting in the car though, and once she was sitting beside me, I quickly got us on the move.

"You know we don't necessarily have to wait until we get to my place," I said casually.

"And what are you suggesting? That we go to my place?"

"That's an option, or we can simply pull over somewhere and utilize the darkness surrounding us," I replied, grinning in the devious way of a cartoon character villain.

"That's... interesting."

The way she spoke those two words gave me goosebumps and had me searching for any side street that looked like it would serve its purpose. A few moments later, I had us parked down a dead-end street, and I was pulling her onto my lap.

"I missed you," she purred, straddling me as she reached a hand into my shorts.

"Right back at you. I was..."

The sudden flash of blue and red lights interrupted what I'd been about to say, along with the mood, causing Tynesha to slide off of my lap and back to her seat. A quick glance in my side mirror revealed an SUV a few feet behind us with the light flashes coming from the grill of the truck.

It could've been a coincidence that we got pulled over not far from Tynesha's mom's house, but coincidence wasn't something I was taught to believe in.

"You might wanna get your phone out and start to record," I said, straightening my clothes while keeping my eyes on my side mirror.

She complied without a word, and we waited in silence for whatever was about to go down. It was a full three minutes before I saw movement come from the truck, and when someone finally stepped out, it wasn't who I expected to see. I lowered my window as the silhouette came closer, but I knew that I wasn't mistaken because the scent of perfume arrived just before she did.

"Sir, may I ask you what you and your passenger are doing parked here?"

"Uh, yes, ma'am. We just pulled over for a minute to discuss our next destination. We were just about to be on our way," I replied.

"Really? Well, it would've been hard to drive with her in your lap, wouldn't it?" she asked, smirking at me before her eyes skated over to Ty.

I rapidly analyzed the pros and cons of lying to this cop versus ignoring her comment and moving this process along. The worst that could happen was a ticket, so it didn't really matter either way.

"Listen, Officer, we were just..."

"Sir, have you been drinking tonight?" she asked abruptly.

'Not enough for either of us to be inebriated," Tynesha said, holding her phone at an angle to get a shot of the cop outside my window.

In response to Tynesha's comment, the cop pulled the flashlight off of her belt and shined its beam first into my eyes and then Tynesha's.

"Sir, I'm gonna need you to step out of the car. Ma'am, you need to stay seated."

I didn't get a chance to offer any response before my door was opened for me, and I was given a look that stated I could come out willingly or not. Despite my frustration, I stepped out of the car while making sure to keep my hands in plain sight. When I was led back to the cop's SUV, I could see Tynesha still holding her phone up and recording the unnecessary bullshit that I was now being subjected to.

"Sir, because I smell alcohol on your breath, I will now administer some routine field sobriety tests, unless you refuse to cooperate."

"Nah, it's fine. Let's just get it over with so that I can be on my way," I replied, frustrated.

As the test began, the flashing lights suddenly got brighter, which signaled that backup had arrived. A few moments later, another female cop stepped on the scene and immediately went to handle Tynesha. I assumed that she was about to be given the same field sobriety tests as me, but when she was pulled from the car, she was immediately handcuffed and forced to sit on the curb. Her phone was put on the roof of my car, so now. all that her Facebook Live followers could see was the beautiful night sky. I was trying to focus on what the other cop was doing, but being asked to balance all of my weight on one foot while touching the tip of my nose with my finger required my full attention. I passed the test with flying colors, which moved us to name reciting the alphabet backwards.

"P-O-N-M..."

"I got a gun here," the other cop announced, interrupting me.

My eyes quickly snapped in her direction, and sure enough, she was holding what looked to be a chrome Taurus .380 by her thumb and index finger.

"Sir, is that your gun or the passenger's?" the cop asked, grabbing my arm as if I'd made a move to flex.

"It's neither of ours," I replied honestly.

I didn't own a .380, and I knew damn well that Tynesha wouldn't be carrying one without telling me about it.

"Well, I found it under her seat, so she goes down for it," the other cop stated.

All it took was for me to look at Tynesha one time to know that the fix was in, and this was a setup, most likely orchestrated by Roland's bitch ass.

"It's my gun, not hers," I said instinctively.

"David, no, I..."

"Shut up, Ty. I'm not letting you cover for me, just because I have priors. It's my gun; it's my charge so let her go."

The feeling of cuffs on my wrists was familiar to me, but I still flinched slightly when they were tightened without warning.

"Sir, you have the right to remain silent..."

Chapter 6

"I'd like to make my phone call now," I stated calmly.

"You must've watched one too many cop shows if you think THAT'S how this works. You'll get the phone when we bring it to you so grab a Snickers," the female arresting officer replied, pushing me down into one of the two chairs occupying the interview room.

Some slick shit to respond with was on the tip of my tongue, but the door was already closing on her disappearing figure. I took a deep breath to steady my nerves, hating the taste of stale recycled air that invaded my mouth but needing to calm myself before the show began. The LAST place my Black ass wanted to be was in police custody given the fact that I'd literally just taken Detective Simms' girl. I was here though and right now, leaving wasn't an option, so I needed to mentally prepare for whatever bullshit was coming my way. I had no doubt that this shit was a setup, which meant that nobody's prints would be on the gun that they 'found' in my car. That would mean little though because as a convicted felon, I didn't get the benefit of doubt. Plus, I had no business being AROUND a gun. Knowing that I had a top-notch attorney on speed dial made me feel better, but he wouldn't be worth a damn until I got to a phone.

"Well, would you look at this?"

I didn't have to turn around to know who was walking into the room because I recognized Roland's voice, even without the same aggression filling it as when I'd last heard it.

"You really must not enjoy having a job because you keep making fucked up, illegal moves that can't be disguised, Detective Simms."

"Disguised? The fact that you think that I have to hide my agenda to nail your bitch ass to the wall shows how ill-equipped you are to deal with me, David. You see, it's not WHAT you know; it's WHO you know, and I know A LOT of people. I know their secrets too, David, and do you know what that means?"

"That you've been reading someone's diary. Or maybe it's that you think you knowing a secret somehow makes you above the law."

My response made him chuckle as he took a seat in the chair across from me and kicked his feet up on the table. Roland wasn't a big dude, but his presence made the windowless room smaller, and I didn't like that feeling. I kept my poker face on though because I'd sooner die than let this hoe nigga see me sweat.

"I don't have to be above the law when I AM the law, but either way, I can do what I want," he bragged.

"Like plant guns on people?"

"I'm offended that you would even make the suggestion that I would stoop so low," he replied, grinning widely.

Had it not been for the fact that my hands were cuffed behind my back, I would've been across the table and on his muthafuckin ass like he owed me money and fucked my bitch. Instead, I was forced to sit and wait while he played out his fifteen minutes of fame.

"I didn't plant any gun nor did I instruct for one to be planted on you. So, that means the gun in question is really yours, or maybe you need to be careful who you allow in your car."

"It's NOT my gun, and the only person in my car with me was my GIRL," I replied, smiling.

The fact that his smile faltered when I mentioned Tynesha as being my girl only made me grin harder. I could tell that he wanted to do something, and his restraint told me that this little impromptu interrogation was definitely being monitored by someone behind the two-way mirror.

"You don't know Tynesha well enough to be calling her your girl, or to assume that she didn't have that gun, so my advice is don't let pussy misguide you."

"Oh, trust me, it hasn't, but it's obvious that you're suffering from pussy withdrawals because you're out here in these streets acting a damn fool. That's so disappointing, Roland. It is GOOD PUSSY though, ain't it? By the way, I think, at this point, it's safe to say that I know Ty REAL well."

My taunting had fire flashing in his eyes as he planted his feet on the floor and stood up. I expected him to either reach across the table and hit me or just come around the muthafucka to do it, but instead, his expression softened a little as he visibly fought for control of himself.

"David, I know that you think that you're doing the right thing, and you're simply protecting her from whatever she told you is going on between us, but I promise you that you're being misled. I don't know exactly WHAT she told you, but I'm sure it wasn't the whole truth."

"Maybe, maybe not. At this point, I'm sure she told me the truth about you because you really don't know how to take a hint, my nigga. She DON'T want you, Roland, and no means no."

"She doesn't want me, huh?" he asked, pulling his phone from his pocket. "Not even a little? Are you sure, Davy boy?"

It seemed like the certainty I spoke with amused him because he was chuckling to himself while doing something on his phone. When he finally slid it across the table to me, I understood why he felt like he knew something that I didn't. I couldn't reach out and pick up the phone, given the fact that my hands were cuffed behind me, but I could clearly read the text messages on the screen.

"Is this supposed to mean something to me?" I asked seriously.

"Well, I'm sure that you can read, David, so you can see that your GIRL messaged me within the last twenty-four hours to apologize to me."

"Okay... and?" I asked, expecting more.

I could immediately tell that my nonchalance was getting under his skin, but he managed to keep his smirk in place.

"Oh, so you don't mind the woman that you're sharing a bed with reaching out to the nigga who's been fucking her faithfully for the past couple years? How long do you think it'll be before she's apologizing in the form of her lips being wrapped around my dick?"

I read the text messages on his phone again to make sure that I hadn't missed anything, and then, I looked back up at him. I could tell by the look in his eyes that he actually believed the shit he was saying, and holding my laughter in was impossible.

"Silly nigga, I can't kick no dick out of her past, and she can't kick no pussy out of mine. Furthermore, I don't know how you got all of that out of this text that does nothing more than apologize for how shit ended between you two but okay. In case you didn't know before now, that's called closure, you lame ass nigga. The big difference between you and me, Roland, is that I'm not trying to handcuff the pussy, so if Tynesha chooses to share it, then that's her choice. I'm confident that my dick game will have her coming back for more, but you're OBVIOUSLY not that confident in your... abilities."

Even though his moves were telegraphed by the contorting of his face, I still didn't duck fast enough to avoid the backhand smack that he hit me with. The wall to my right stopped me from landing in the floor, but it still hurt to bounce off of it, and the taste of blood in my mouth made me want to kill this nigga. The sound of someone tapping from the other side of the mirror behind him prevented me from doing more than chuckling as I struggled to sit back upright in my seat.

"So sensitive, Detective Simms. If it's a performance issue that really made Tynesha leave you, you know the wonders of medicine have improved dramatically, so you don't have to be ashamed."

"If there weren't eyes on us right now, I'd show you just how well my dick works, you pussy," he growled, scooping up his phone and putting it back in his pocket.

"Ah, I get now... you're having QUESTIONS about your sexual preferences? NOW I understand why she was starving for my GOOD LOVING and why she's not with you. What happened? Did she catch you watching a little backdoor bandit, male on male porn before you hopped in the bed with her?"

I knew that his better judgement had to be screaming at him, but he still grabbed me up by my throat and slammed me up against the wall. This time, the sound coming from behind the two-way mirror was an unmistakable pounding, and it was accompanied by a similar sound from the door next to us.

"Your young ass is gonna die for being stupid. Mark my words," his whispered fiercely before releasing his hold on me.

"You should be careful who you wish death on because the Grim Reaper doesn't discriminate. You might find yourself a victim, OFFICER Simms. I mean, your job is very dangerous."

"You're speaking my language, little nigga, so whenever you're ready..."

The door suddenly opening caused him to stop speaking and take a step back, but the tension in the air made misinterpreting what was going on an impossibility.

"Detective Simms, I'd like a moment alone with my client."

Hearing the unfamiliar voice of a woman referring to me forced me to break the staring contest we'd been having and look over at the petite, white woman standing in the doorway. Her face was attractive, even though it was obviously all business. I'd never seen the short, brown haired, brown eyed woman looking through the Gucci framed glasses at Roland with blatant impatience, but her referring to me as her client brought comfort in uncertain times.

"I'll see you soon," Roland said, winking at me before moving away from me and out the door.

"I'm sure that that experience was as friendly as it looked, wasn't it?"

"Just another day of being a Black man in America. Guilty until proven innocent," I replied, calmly retaking my seat.

Once she closed the door, she took the seat across from me, sitting her briefcase on the table in between us.

"Mr. Bishop, my name is Carrie Bask. I represent a law firm out of Ft. Lauderdale, and I was contacted by a mutual friend of ours to come down here and see about your case."

"I appreciate you getting here so quickly," I said, smiling so that she could see the blood that I was tasting filling my mouth and sliding down my throat.

She looked at me calmly for a few seconds before deliberately looking at the two-way mirror.

"Make sure I get a copy of the tape from the time that my client stepped foot into this room with Detective Simms up until the moment I entered," she demanded.

No response came, but she and I knew that someone had heard her words.

"David, I want you to take me back a few hours and tell me what happened after you left your condo."

I quickly ran down our dinner plans, making sure to leave out the part where I mistakenly got head from Tynesha's twin sister, Tesha. Carrie didn't take any notes, but I could tell by the expression on her face that she was listening intently. Once I recapped the events of the evening, she opened her briefcase and pulled out a sheet of paper that I recognized, even looking at it upside down.

"The good news is that there's no gunshot residue on your hands or clothing, and your prints shouldn't come back on the gun based on your version of what happened. The bad news is that your record paints an unflattering picture of you because you have three assaults, a malicious wounding, and a separate conviction for possession of a firearm," she explained.

"The first gun charge was a fluke because I took it from my homeboy to keep him from doing something stupid that night. I just happened to get stopped and searched that night for driving while Black."

"And the history of assaults?" she asked.

I had no answer to give her except for that some niggas just needed their ass whooped to remind them that their actions had consequences. As logical as that was to me, I didn't think this nice lady would agree or understand.

"I'm not judging you, David, but I do want you to know how the system and society views violent felons because they look for patterns to determine escalation."

"I get it, but I'm telling you that gun they found doesn't belong to me or Ty."

She put the paper containing my record aside and leaned across the table toward me.

"I know that this was all Roland's doing, but you gotta be able to see past that to his next move. Anticipate it and get in front of it," she whispered.

Her words instantly filled my mind with thoughts of Tynesha and the possible harm this pussy nigga could try to inflict. I wasn't having it though, and I didn't believe the nigga was off limits just because he carried a badge. It was time to get on some NWA shit and scream fuck the police.

"How long will it take to get me out?" I asked, feeling a sense of urgency and impatience.

"That's a very good question. Sit tight while I find out."

She got up from the table and left the room, leaving me alone with my thoughts. I could feel my anger slowly building, but I had it under control because I understood that reckless moves weren't what I needed right now. My young age didn't stop me from fully analyzing a situation, but I knew it made a nigga like Roland underestimate me. Even though I knew that I couldn't trust a word that came out of the crooked ass detective's mouth, I was now wondering what secrets Tynesha did have. Everyone had secrets, and no one knew that better than me, which was why I wasn't in a position to judge. If I was going to die and kill behind this girl, then I needed to know EVERYTHING, and I knew where to start looking for those answers. The outlines of a plan began to formulate in my mind, and I chewed on it for twenty minutes until two familiar faces came back through the door of the interview room.

"Good news, David, the Orlando police department has agreed to let you off with a citation for now, which means you'll have to appear for a court date at some point. Right now, you're free to go," Carrie said, smiling brightly.

While she'd been explaining, Officer Leonard had been removing the handcuffs, and it felt good to be able to move my broad shoulders freely again. When I stood up, I towered over the cop who couldn't have been more than 5'7" standing next to Carrie's 5'6". Even though he looked physically fit, I still knew that I could break his jaw with one punch. The thought made me smile.

"Still playing flunky, huh, Officer Leonard?" I asked.

"Fuck you," he replied under his breath before leaving the room.

"Let's get you out of here," Carrie said.

It took about fifteen minutes to process me out at the front desk, but once I was out front of the police station, breathing fresh air, I felt rejuvenated.

"Carrie, I appreciate you coming through and getting me out. Send me an invoice for your bill."

"Don't worry about it. Tynesha is my girl. Plus, I'm not ACTUALLY a lawyer. I'm just a secretary at a law firm part time, which is why I chose my words carefully," she replied, smiling mischievously.

I chuckled even as I scanned our surroundings to make sure there was nobody around to overhear our conversation.

"However you did it, I still appreciate it because you didn't have to come down here at all. If there's ever anything I can do for you, just let me know."

"So... you wanna owe me a favor?" she asked softly.

For a half a second, I thought she was flirting, but I chalked it up to my overactive imagination.

"Yeah, I owe you."

"I'm gonna hold you to those words, David. Do you need me to drop you off anywhere?" She offered.

"Nah, I'm good," I replied, pulling my phone out.

She gave a sexy wave as she walked away toward the parking lot, and for a second, my eyes got stuck on her ass because I didn't expect this white girl to be that thick. I had to shake that off though because there was pressing business to attend to. I arranged for a Lyft to pick me up a couple blocks from the police station because it didn't make sense to stand out front when Carrie had just run a vicious bluff to get me out.

Within fifteen minutes, I was secured in the back of a blue Ford Explorer driven by a heavyset white boy that looked a few years older than me. When asked for the destination I wanted to go to, I surprised myself with the address I rattled off, but deep down, I knew I wouldn't sleep until I had some answers. It took us another twenty minutes before the truck crept to a stop on the dark and deserted street, and I hopped out to the sounds of the night's insects singing in concert. I wasted no time going around the back of Tynesha's mom's house, thanking my lucky stars that one of my niggas had dated Tesha in high school, and he'd told me about sneaking out of her window on the first floor.

My luck held because she wasn't sleep, and her bedroom light was on. I tapped on the window lightly, but she still jumped high enough to give a scared cat acrobatic lessons. I was too busy laughing softly to see her hand disappear out of sight, but when she pulled the curtain back, I found myself looking down the barrel of a pretty, pink Glock .42. The laughter died in my throat immediately. My hands shot up out of reflex, and I was relieved to see recognition cloud her green eyes.

"Negro, are you trying to die tonight?" she asked once the window was open.

"Hell nah, but I need to talk to you. It's important."

"What the fuck could be so important as to have you knocking at my window at this time of night, boy?" she asked skeptically.

"Let me in and I'll explain."

For a few seconds, she just stared at me, but then, she backed up and motioned me forward. A voice in the back of my mind was wondering loudly if this was my second mistake with this woman tonight, but it was too late to analyze.

Chapter 7

I didn't dare invite myself to sit on her king-sized bed, and based on what had happened earlier between us, I knew it was best to keep my distance.

"After me and Ty left here, we got pulled over by some cops and…"

"And they found a gun in your car. I know because she called me, crying in frustration," Tesha said, shaking her head while putting her gun back under her mattress.

"Well, when I got down to the police station, Roland showed his face and made some threats."

"You shouldn't take his words as threats because they're more than that. If he said it then he MEANT IT, and that muthafucka is for real dangerous," she stated seriously.

For a moment, I was taken aback by how well she seemed to know her sister's ex because I was under the impression that Tynesha had kept her mom and sister in the dark about Roland's bullshit. Something wasn't adding up for me.

"You talk like you KNOW this nigga, Tesha. How and why do you know this nigga is what I'm wondering?" I admitted.

"Not as well as I know you so don't sound too jealous, boo. I would NEVER let that nigga touch me, taste me, or do anything like that."

"Okay, so how do you know him?" I persisted.

"Info ain't free, David, and you know that. What's in it for me? And don't act like what you're asking ain't important because you wouldn't be sneaking around in the dark like this. Shit, I bet my life that my sister has no idea that you're here right now."

"Nah, she don't, and she don't need to know," I said, making my meaning clear with a pointed look.

"My lips are sealed."

The malicious smile that spread across her face momentarily altered her beauty, but it didn't surprise me because I'd always known that Tesha was the twin who was with the shit.

"So, what is it that you want, Tesha?"

"I think you already know the answer to that question," she replied, pulling her oversized, black, T-shirt off over her head.

She stood there, naked, and it was IMPOSSIBLE for me not to look at her, even though I tried to play it cool.

"You know I'm fucking with your sister, and I really want that to turn into something serious."

"I hear that, and I ain't even trying to get in the way of your little love connection, but she wasn't the only one who wanted to know what the dick was hittin for. This stays between us. I promise," she said seductively, moving slowly in my direction.

It wasn't until she was standing right in front of me that my eyes actually left her body and refocused on her face. I'd been looking for any distinguishable differences between her and Ty, but they really were a beautiful set of identical twins. My mind and heart knew that this was all kinds of wrong, but my hard dick could care less about my morals being compromised at this point.

"Tesha, we can't…"

"Shhhh and stop overthinking this because I know you ain't scared of a little more pussy being added to your menu. Come here," she demanded, taking my hand and leading me over to her bed.

She pushed me onto my back and climbed on top of me, wasting no time going for my zipper.

"I-I don't have a condom," I said in a last-ditch effort to pause the inevitable.

"Neither do I but that's what birth control and Plan Bs are for."

No more words got the chance to pass my lips before she maneuvered herself over top of me and slid down my dick like she'd been a firefighter all her life. The breath was pushed from my lungs in a familiar way, but she breathed for me with a toe-curling kiss. I was in a daze from the heat of her pussy alone, but it was the grip that accompanied that warm wetness that almost made me pass the fuck out. She rode me slowly, deliberately at first, which made everything worse in the best possible way. All I could do was hold on to her waist while fighting for control of the heart that was beating wildly in my chest. She tasted like delicious sin dipped in sugar, and I indulged by kissing her with an unchecked fierceness that only made her pussy wetter. When she bit my lip, I felt a chill race through my body like electric currents were suddenly a part of my genetic DNA, and it brought to life Frankenstein's monster inside of me.

I quickly rolled her onto her back while tossing her long, limber, left leg up onto my right shoulder, and then, I dove inside her with the perfection of a seasoned sky diver who knew no fear. Her waves pushed back against my invasion, smashing against my rock-hard dick loud enough to bring the sea creatures out of hiding. I swiftly set the rhythm to pound on repeat while covering her mouth with my hand to muffle the sounds of her passion. The more I put my back into it, wanting and needing to deliver sweet punishment, the wetter she got and the more her eyes rolled. I could feel the tension building within her taunt body, and I decided to up the ante. In a quick move, I rolled her onto her side which put her left leg on my other shoulder and allowed my fingers to rub her clit in a circular motion, as I continued slamming my dick deep inside her pussy.

"Shit!" She squealed loudly before using both of her own hands to clamp her mouth shut.

I fucked her steadily, losing myself within her maze, until we both came in sounds strangled grunts and unintelligible moans. I came so hard that my knees gave out, forcing me to release my hold on her and collapse beside her. We sucked in air in great gulps for at least five minutes without attempting to pass a word between us, exhausted but undeniably satisfied.

"I s-see why she didn't come up for air for a week," Tesha said, giggling.

"Do me a favor and DON'T bring up your sister right after I just fucked you."

"Fair enough," she replied, sitting up and grabbing a wooden jewelry box off of her nightstand.

A few moments later, the scent of good weed took to the air and hung over us like Los Angeles smog. I started not to take the blunt when she passed it to me, but I ended up saying fuck it and filling my lungs with some of the good gas.

"So, what do you know about Roland?" I asked, steering us back to the business I'd come for before she made me cum.

"Well... how much do you wanna know?"

"I wanna know what you know," I replied, passing her the blunt back.

She took a few pulls before putting it out and lying back down beside me.

"He was born and raised in the Pork and Beans projects. He got his feet wet in the game by drug running for the Haitians and Zoe Pound, but that didn't last long because he became their hired gun. They pointed him at their Cuban competition, and he made more muthafuckas disappear than Covid-19 when it first hit. One day, someone high up in the Zoe Pound organization decided that Roland was smart enough, and slippery enough, to infiltrate the police force. It turned out that was the right call to make. Roland could never be Zoe Pound because he's not Haitian, but he made himself indispensable by being a good cop who was really bad. He's been that ever since. He has his hands in drugs, girls, guns. I mean, you name it, and he's either on the inside or at the door for all major plays in Florida. If you were looking for a formidable opponent then congratulations because you've got the class valedictorian on your hands," she said.

The tone of her voice had been deadpan and straightforward, but it was also undoubtedly honest. I didn't respond right away, choosing to process these revelations in silence to better hear what my instincts and intuition were going to tell me. I feared no one, but I knew the advantages to being aware of my opps' capabilities. From the sound of shit, I was either going to have to let Tynesha go or be willing to go all in about her. It wasn't a question of whether or not she was worth it because I knew she was. The question was how would this affect the shit that I was into that I kept a secret? I knew somewhere down the line that my path intersected with Roland's, and not just because of Ty. I could figure all of that out later though. Right now, I needed to focus on finding this nigga's weaknesses.

"What I don't understand is why YOU know all of this and why your sister didn't tell me none of it when we talked," I said, turning on my side so that I could study Tesha's face.

"Ty didn't tell you because she doesn't know, and before you ask, I didn't tell her because he would've killed her if she was unwilling to accept him as he really is. Deep down, he's an insecure man with a fragile ego, which makes him even MORE dangerous, and that's why I kept her safely in the dark. The reason that I know so much is because I make it my business to know the people I'm forced into business with."

Her statement was nonchalant, but there was no WAY what she'd said was getting past me.

"How the fuck would you find yourself in business with this kind of nigga?" I asked curiously.

"He ran down on a nigga I was dating who sold dope, and he made him disappear, but he couldn't bring himself to kill me... one of the benefits of having the same face as the woman he's obsessed with."

"So, what business do you and him have now?" I asked, confused.

"I sell dope for him, which is part of the reason I'm going back to school, so that I can expand his clientele."

Disbelief froze any words I was going to speak, but I got over it quickly enough.

"What makes you think he's obsessed with Ty?" I asked, changing thought processes.

"He slipped up and mentioned seeing her play in a high school volleyball tournament, which told me that he's had eyes on her since she was at least sixteen years old. Long before they HAPPENED to bump into each other at the club. If that wasn't enough of a red flag, there's the shit he does to Ty. She thought I didn't know about the abuse, but she's my twin, and I know her just like she knows me. Plus, I did volunteer work at a battered woman's shelter called Guests of Florida, so I know what a woman going through abuse looks like."

"Why the fuck didn't you stop her from fucking with this nigga?" I asked, sitting up in the bed.

I expected some type of half-assed excuse to come out of her mouth in justification, but all I got was silence instead. When I looked back at her, I could see the tears welling up in her eyes, and it made me pause for a second. As I looked at her closer though, I saw more than tears. I saw fear.

"Tesha, what aren't you telling me?"

"What do you mean? I told you everything that I know about the nigga, Roland," she replied defensively.

"Okay, but it's something that you're not telling me, and I know because I can see the fear in your eyes. Obviously, you trust me a little so talk to me. I'm not judging you."

"I don't care if you judge me. It's just... I was so fucking STUPID, David! I made a deal with the devil."

"What does that mean?" I asked hesitantly.

"The boyfriend that I was with that Roland made disappear was shot, and... and Roland made me put my prints on the gun that he was shot with. He still has that gun as an insurance plan, and he never lets me forget that he owns me."

"Oh, fuck," I mumbled.

"It gets worse because the nigga he killed was somebody kinda important... He was the governor's son."

Chapter 8

I'd lost track of time, aimlessly walking the streets of Orlando after leaving Tesha's bedroom, but I'd needed to clear my head and process the new information with the old. I was no stranger to getting into it with a nigga, but Tesha's words about how formidable Roland was were still ringing in my ears kind of loud. I wasn't afraid of him per se; it was more so the fear of the extremes I'd have to go to in order to truly eliminate this nigga as a threat. For all I knew, killing him could make other threats pop up, and then, it was all out warfare for real. The blood that I had on my hands from the things I'd done in the past was the kind that washed off after a thorough scrubbing. If I took a run at Roland, something told me that I'd never be clean again. It was this knowledge that had kept my feet moving for hours until I finally found myself at my front door with the rising sun accompanying me. I didn't have my keys because Tynesha had stayed with my car, so it was times like this that made me glad I'd invested in modern technology. A couple years back, I'd had a microchip implanted into my hand that allowed me to swipe a panel next to my door's lock and unlock every lock attached to the door. Before I could put my hand to it now, I heard Stoney barking excitedly, and I physically braced for impact. As soon as the door was open wide enough for her massive head to fit through, she shot through the gap like a seasoned running back and slammed her whole body into me.

"I missed you too. Now quit it," I said, laughing while playing with her and scratching behind her ears.

I could feel someone staring at me, and I looked up to find Tynesha a few feet away, wearing one of my t-shirts and holding the two-tone Taurus 9mm I kept under my pillow firmly in her grip. I could tell by the look in her eyes that she'd been crying, and she was running on little to no sleep, just like I was. Even in my sleep deprived state though, I could feel the tension between us, and my mind automatically flipped back to the moments I'd just spent with Tesha. If she hadn't kept that secret, then there was little doubt in my mind when it came to me living on borrowed time.

"Where have you been?" she asked softly.

"Walking around, trying to clear my head."

"All night? Do you know how worried and scared I've been, especially because Carrie texted me after she got you out? I thought something had happened to you," she said, her anger becoming more apparent in her breathing.

I didn't say anything at first, but instead, I stepped completely inside my condo so that nosy neighbors wouldn't happen upon whatever this scene turned out to be. Stoney could sense that something was wrong because she stopped trying to play and instead just sat down beside me, facing toward Tynesha. She wasn't being aggressive or growling low in her throat, but I knew my dog well enough to know that she was prepared to attack any threat.

"I wasn't trying to worry you, Ty. I was just trying to figure shit out and make it make sense. I'm sorry that I didn't call you or text you that."

"You're sorry, huh? Are you sorry about having a gun in your car and not telling me too? I found this one tucked underneath your pillow when I laid down, which explains why you always sleep on the right side of the bed," she replied, holding up the gun for me to see.

"The gun you're holding is mine, and there are a few others stashed around the house too, but the one the cops 'found' in my car wasn't one of mine. Don't you think that I would've made a move to get rid of it or at least have it on me so that they wouldn't even suspect you?"

I could tell by the look in her eyes that she'd considered the same thing at some point between when we'd gotten pulled over and now, so I didn't know why she was questioning me like this.

"It wasn't my gun either, and I never would've let you go to jail for me if it was mine. Seriously, David, I…"

"I know that. Roland couldn't help but to come and gloat as soon as he knew that I was secured in the police station," I said, shaking my head disgustedly.

"So, it WAS Roland, which means…"

Her voice trailed off, but I could see the understanding in her eyes as clear as the sun still rising outside. I knew that she was afraid of Roland already but for different reasons than she'd be if I'd told her everything that I'd learned from her sister about this nigga. I wasn't trying to terrify her for any reason. I just didn't want to have all of these lies between us. The only solution that I could come up with was to stand on half-truths and pray for forgiveness later.

"Ty, I need you to stay away from Roland. No communication, no nothing."

"You say that like I've got a lunch date set with this nigga or something," she replied, not bothering to hide her irritation.

"Nah, I said it like that apology you offered didn't have the positive affect that you wanted."

She didn't hide her surprise well, and I didn't want her to. I'd wanted to put her on defense to avoid any scrutiny of how I'd spent the last few hours.

"I'm gonna grab a quick shower, and then, we need to talk," I said, moving toward her.

With all the walking I'd done, I was sure that I smelled more like outside and sweat than what Tesha and I had done, but I wasn't taking any chances, so I dropped a quick kiss on Ty's forehead and kept it moving.

"Stay, Stoney," Ty commanded.

To my surprise, Stoney sat right at her feet, and for some reason, that made me smile all the way to the shower. I spent a quick twenty minutes washing the jail off of me, as well as the sins I knew I'd have to take to the grave with me. Getting my dick sucked by Tesha had been an honest mistake that could've happened to anybody, but there was no excuse or justification acceptable for me fucking her. I wasn't even going to waste time in my own mind trying to make that part make sense, so all my focus went into the big problem in front of me. Detective Roland Simms. When I walked into my bedroom from the shower, I could smell food immediately, and the shots my stomach took at me let me know that ignoring it wasn't an option. I quickly threw on a pair of boxer briefs and some shorts before walking into the kitchen where I found Ty looking effortlessly sexy concentrating over a hot stove.

"What's on the menu?" I asked, walking up behind her.

She glanced over her shoulder at me and smiled.

"YOU if you don't put a damn shirt on! As for what I'm cooking, well, that's just a little hero's welcome of pancakes, eggs, sausage, and fried potatoes."

"You put onions in the potatoes?" I asked, hopeful.

"Boy, don't be disrespectful. Who the hell fries potatoes without the onions?"

I quickly held my hands up in surrender and acknowledgement of my blasphemous question while hopping up on the counter beside the refrigerator and taking a seat.

"You gonna look over my shoulder now to make sure I don't fuck up? Don't MAKE ME call my mama because she's the one who taught me how to cook," she threatened playfully.

"Baby, I don't doubt your skills in the slightest, but I figured that we could talk while you cook."

"Oh... Okay," she replied cautiously.

"So, I reached out to some of my people after I got out, just trying to get a better read on this nigga, Roland, because it's obvious that we're enemies at this point. I was warned that he's formidable."

"Because he's a cop?" she asked.

"Because he's a DIRTY cop with ties to Zoe Pound, and he's not playing by any rules other than the ones he's making."

"Zoe Pound? As in them Haitians?" she asked, turning to look at me in a strange way.

"Yeah, he grew up under their thumb, and from what I hear, it was them who told him to be a cop."

"Makes sense since law enforcement is THE BIGGEST gang in the world. What you said also explains why I've walked in on him having conversations in the French dialect that Haitians speak down here. What does all of this mean though?" she asked.

"It means that this shit is realer than the pandemic when it swept across the world."

I watched as she processed that statement before she turned back around to the stove. The sounds of grease popping filled the kitchen, and it would've been easy to let the conversation die or switch topics, but I owed her better than that.

"There could be a bigger problem," I stated slowly.

"How is that even possible?"

"Because if Roland is now who I believe him to be, then he'll know some of my associates that I do business with," I replied vaguely.

My words caused her to stop cooking and turn around completely to face me.

"Who the hell are you associating with that could be connected to HIS bullshit, David?"

"When you asked me about the work I do, I told you that I do 'a little this and that,' but I'm a full-time personal trainer. The THIS and THAT part of that statement involves illegal activities, mainly scamming."

"Scamming?" she replied quizzically.

"Yeah. Checks, credit cards, gift cards, merchandise scams, selling knockoffs, fake government loans, and a variety of other things that I can do with a few keystrokes from my laptop."

"You always were good with computers in school... but I still don't understand where Roland fits in," she said.

"I'm plugged into the criminal element out here, and I have a reputation of sorts that's bad in a good way. The more that Roland digs into me and my past, looking for weaknesses to exploit, the higher the odds get that he finds out what I'm into now. When that happens, he can either try to set me up to get me locked up on some shit that'll stick to my ribs like home cooking, or he can fuck up my business by making my friends my enemies."

"Would your people really turn on you for him?" she asked naïvely.

"Loyalty is often brought in these types of situations, and they would fear Roland more than me because he can hide behind his badge and make killing legal."

The understanding in her eyes magnified at the same rate as her fear, but I didn't catch a glimpse of its pinnacle because she turned back to the stove. She cooked in silence as the air continued filling with the smells of amazing foods that were fighting for dominance over the weight of my revelations hanging in the air. I had no doubt that she probably felt betrayed to some degree because I hadn't been one hundred percent honest with her about the way my life was set up right now. I just didn't want those thoughts and feelings to morph into her doubting herself when it came to her ability to pick a good man over a bad one. In my heart, I knew that I was a good man with the potential to be great, but I was a man with demons like many men who came before me. I knew that I needed to give her a minute to work through what I'd just unloaded on her, but the feeling of insecurity was filling my chest rapidly like I was trying to drink the ocean.

"Ty... baby, talk to me please."

"And say what?"

"I don't know… I just know that I don't want to lose you behind this shit. I'm not scared of Roland or any nigga he can get to side with him. I'm ONLY afraid of losing you and what we're building," I confessed vulnerably.

She didn't immediately respond to what I said, instead finishing up putting the fried potatoes on our plates with the rest of the food. When she carried the plates into the dining room, I followed her, as obedient and loyal as Stoney was, without saying another word. We sat at opposite ends of the table with the orange juice and condiments between us to go along with enough emotional space to drop the Grand Canyon into it. I wanted to speak, but I chose to wait because I refused to push her in either direction.

"Do you have a plan?" she asked, finally looking at me across the table.

"Not really. All I know is that he has to die because that's the only thing that will stop him from coming after you."

"And you're okay with that? Taking a life, I mean?" she asked.

"For you I'd do it without question or hesitation."

For a moment, she stared through me, and I didn't know what she was looking at or how it would affect us in the end. Suddenly, she began singing in a surprisingly beautiful tone.

"Cross my heart and hope to die. To my lover, I'd never lie. He said, 'be true,' I said, 'I'll try.' In the end, it's him and I. He's out his head; I'm out my mind. We got that good love, the crazy kind. I am his, and he is mine. In the end, it's him and I. Him and I," she sang softly.

I could feel the hair on my arms rise up as my mind scrambled to place the familiar tune and the powerful lyrics. I knew I'd heard it before, and my mind suddenly flashed back to senior prom. It was one of the songs that the DJ had played that night, the last night that I'd been close enough to smell cucumber melon on Tynesha's skin before our paths had crossed at the gas station days ago. Despite having a date of my own that prom night, I'd still had to acknowledge Ty's beauty, and if the look I was seeing in her eyes right now was what I thought it was, then that meant she remembered that night as well.

"That's the song *Him & I* by G-Eazy and Halsey," I said.

"It is. And now, you know where I stand. Just be true to me, David, always, because I can't handle another heartbreak."

The sincerity she spoke with was hard to miss or misinterpret, which made my heart beat faster.

"I got you, Ty. Always."

Chapter 9
Three Days Later

If anybody asked me about my childhood, I'd say that I came from a good home for the most part. Being raised by strong Black women in the form of my mother and my grandmother meant that I didn't know the side effects of not having a male role model until I was on the threshold of manhood myself. I was raised as a hustler second and a protector first because a real man knew how to make his woman feel safe while also providing for her wants and needs. These lessons weren't ON ME; they were IN ME, and once I knew that Tynesha was down for the ride, I was allowed to tap into my old self in search of ways to eliminate this problem of her ex-boyfriend. Going against a cop could be considered suicidal by any person of limited intelligence but to be actually actively planning to remove a cop from the face of the earth was pure madness and lunacy. I knew and understood this, but what was love if not a form of madness and lunacy to be consumed by? To fall in love with someone meant adding sacrifice to the mixture of everything else that was already being felt by you. I knew I was on the verge of falling for Ty, despite my brief indiscretion with Tesha, and I wasn't afraid of what I was feeling. I just had to remember not to let it cloud my judgement in the form of making me desperate to kill Roland before the perfect opportunity presented itself. Right now, I was still in the research stage of planning, but I was ready to remove the first piece off of the board.

I'd been parked on a sleepy, dark street for the past hour, blending into the background as I watched a one-story house that sat on the corner in the shadows. The house belonged to the nigga who'd been in the passenger seat the day that Roland had ran down on Tynesha and me at the gas station. I hadn't paid too much attention to him considering the fact that he'd run away like a little bitch but mentioning him to Ty the other night had revealed that the nigga was actually Roland's nephew. Based on his actions, I had him figured as a weak nigga that was possible to exploit, so I'd had Ty run his résumé down to me which led me to sitting outside his house currently. His government name was Quander, but the streets called him Q. He was a part time heroin distributor, but he was a full-time heroin user, which was bad math when it came to playing the game to win. The spot he lived in was also where he trapped out of, but his operation was sloppy, and I'd witnessed that first-hand in the last hour. A few times, I'd seen the fake pretty boy, Q, step his light skin ass out on the porch and conduct a few hand-to-hand sales. He must've thought the laws had changed to make heroin sales legal because he wasn't even trying to hide the fact that he was slanging dope. Maybe that was one of the side effects of having an uncle on the police force, especially because Roland was undoubtedly his connect for the dope too. My first thought was to bring Tesha in on my plan because it would've been impossible for her not to know this nigga, Q, but I wasn't trying to pay the toll she was sure to charge for me being anywhere near her.

So, here I was, dressed in all-black with a throw away, black Glock .27 holding thirty-three shots tucked into my pants, waiting on my moment. The moment that I saw the big butt white girl walking slowly past my car window, I knew that the moment had arrived, and I wasted no time hopping out. It was a warm night with no type of breeze blowing which *could've* explained why this chick was walking down the sidewalk in some skimpy, black lingerie in matching six-inch, stiletto heels. My guess though was that she was coming to get her fix, and pussy was the credit card accepted worldwide. I fell into step with her, but she was oblivious as she led the way to the dope man's front door. When she climbed the steps of the front porch, I blended in with the shadows and made my way around the back of the house.

The level of this nigga's comfort was immediately made clear by the fact that the back door to his house was open, leaving nothing except for a flimsy screen door to keep the boogie man outside. On tip toe, I crept up to the screen and peeked inside, scanning everything between the dirty kitchen and the front door. I could hear music playing softly, and that was the only voice drifting on the stale air out into the night, but I didn't know how many people were actually inside. Q suddenly came into view as he walked to the front door, and a few seconds later, I got to see the face of the chick I'd been following up the sidewalk. She wasn't a head turner when it came to her actual beauty, but the nigga, Q, was on her like she was model material. Once I saw them disappear from view, I slowly eased the screen door open and crept into the house. My nose was immediately assaulted by the strong smells of body odor and cat piss. The latter smell told the story that Q might just be cooking Methamphetamine because I didn't see any signs of animals.

I pulled my pistol out as I made my way up the hallway, unsure of what to expect. The first thing I did was check the three bedrooms in the house to see if anyone else was here. I didn't want to get hit with a surprise bullet to the back of the head because I was sloppy and underestimated my opp. After that was done, I went in search of the main event, which wasn't hard to find because the music had changed and got louder too. When I peeked into the living room, Q was seated on a shit brown, leather couch that was cracked and worn, tossing money at the white girl standing on top of a chipped wooden table, swaying from side to side. Trey Songz had shorty in a zone, and she was moving her body like this was an audition to work at Magic City. Q was all eyes, locked in on the show, but I was unimpressed and focused as I crept all the way into the room. He didn't realize I was there until I sat on the couch next to him and put my pistol to his left temple.

"You don't gotta stop dancing, sweetheart. You're still gonna get paid," I assured her when her movements froze.

The fear filling her blue eyes didn't lessen with my reassurances, but my focus shifted to my reason for being here.

"Do you remember me, Q? I know that you only saw me for a few seconds before you took off running like the scared bitch that you are, but we met at the gas station. Actually, we didn't OFFICALLY meet, so I decided to drop by real quick and say hi."

"What do you want?" he asked, sounding defeated but keeping a neutral expression on his face.

"Just some information. For starters, where is your stash spot?"

He didn't readily reply, which forced me to press the gun barrel to his face a little harder.

"Is it worth dying for?" I asked calmly.

"Bedroom closet in the floor safe. 6-2-2-8-4 is the combination," he replied reluctantly.

"Did you hear that, sweetheart?" I asked, looking at her frozen on top of the table.

She nodded shakily, but I could see the confusion in her eyes.

"Go get it, leave out the back door, and remember that you were NEVER here. Understand?" I asked.

Just like that, the confusion vanished, and she came down off the table like a track star sprinting down the back stretch.

"Now that we're alone, Q, let's get down to the real reason for me being here tonight. I'm here about your Uncle Roland."

"He's gonna kill you."

"Don't go spoiling the ending of the movie, my nigga. We'll get to who lives and who dies soon enough. I need you to tell me where his base of operations is for the drug enterprise that he's managing," I said.

"Nigga, I don't know what you're talking about. My uncle is a cop, not a dope boy."

I calmly lowered the gun away from his temple, put it on his thigh, just above the knee, and I pulled the trigger. Blood and bone fragments blew onto the coffee table like a lover's kiss, but his screams silenced any ideas one might have about this being pleasurable.

"I don't like liars, Q, and I hate muthafuckas who waste my time. That's your first and last warning shot because the next bullet is gonna blow your mind. Literally."

"Wh-what the FUCK do you w-want?!"

"All I want is the location of your uncle's main stash house," I replied.

"He doesn't-he doesn't have one because he doesn't deal with the dope like that. He keeps the m-money in police lockers and drops it off e-every two weeks to the connect," Q stammered, crying openly at this point.

What he was saying made a certain amount of sense because there was less risk in handling money versus dope. It said a lot that the Haitians would trust that nigga with large amounts of currency, but this was some information I could definitely use to my advantage because trust was a fragile thing. When money was involved, your friends could become your opps in the blink of an eye.

"What day is the money drop?" I asked, moving the gun back to his temple.

"I-I don't know; the days change. He moves when they c-call him."

Again, I heard more truth in his words, but I doubted there was much more useful information he could provide. I knew who could connect the rest of the dots for me though.

"Q, I appreciate your time, and I'm sorry that I shot you in the leg like that. I gotta work on my anger management a little more. We're good though, right?"

"I-I need a hospital," he mumbled weakly.

"A hospital? Nah, my nigga, you don't need no hospital. God's got you," I replied sincerely, pulling the trigger one more time.

His body jerked violently to his right, no doubt chasing the thoughts now staining the worn couch next to him. I got up and left him alone with the musical stylistics of Trey Songz carrying him in to glory as I made my way back to my car using the same route I'd snuck in through. Thoughts of burning Q's house to the ground crossed my mind as a way to destroy any and all evidence, but I didn't want to draw that type of attention here. I had gloves on, so I wasn't worried about my prints being left behind, and despite the white girl seeing me there, she'd never seen me in action. No doubt she was too preoccupied with the robbery she'd just pulled off to give a good goddamn about the bitch ass drug dealer who had exploited her addiction for sex.

The main reason that I didn't burn the house down though was because it was my hope that Roland would find his nephew slumped. If that happened, he'd run through all the possible suspects of who could've done it, but somewhere in the back of his mind, he'd see my face and hear my voice. Then, he'd wonder. Warfare was only ten percent physical because it was ninety percent mental, and I knew how to play all parts of the game very well. My goal tonight had been accomplished because I had new information, but I'd also succeeded in making this thing more personal for Roland, and that was sure to be a distraction in the days to come.

Meanwhile, it was time to pull at the fabric of his alliance and see if Zoe Pound was really behind him. When I pulled off into the still growing darkness, I pointed my car in the direction of my condo while texting Ty to let her know that I was on my way. I sent another text message too, knowing that it was my best move, and that concluded my business for the night. It took me a little more than half an hour to make it back home, and as expected, Ty and Stoney were sitting on the couch, waiting for me. I hadn't told her where I was going when I'd left earlier, or what I was doing, because I'd wanted to protect her from as much as I could. After tonight though, I knew that it was time she learned the WHOLE truth so that it wasn't used as a weapon later on. Plus, Ty had valuable knowledge that she didn't realize she had just because she knew this nigga, Roland's, day to day life.

"You okay?" she asked, looking at me from head to toe in the dimly lit living room light.

"I'm good, bae. How bout you?"

"Honestly... I'm worried, David. I don't wanna lose you, and I don't wanna be the reason that you lose yourself. I'm worth a lot, but that's too high of a price for anyone to pay," she said softly.

"You let me be the judge of that, sweetheart, and just keep loving me the way that you do. I promise that I'm not losing myself, and you're definitely not losing me. I do what I do for us and for our future because nothing and no one can stand in the way of that. I put that on God."

Chapter 10

"David... Baby, I'm not perfect, and I pray that you don't see me as such. Please don't put me on that pedestal because I'm only gonna disappoint you like I do everyone else."

"Bae, I deal with reality, so I KNOW you're not perfect, and neither am I. You can be perfect for me though, and I can be the same for you as long as we put our best foot forward in this relationship," I replied sincerely.

"I agree... and I'm sorry that I didn't talk to you before I texted Roland, but..."

"Ty, you can STOP apologizing for that because I'm not mad about that part. I told you that I respect the fact that you tried to give the nigga closure and move on smoothly, but he can't handle it. You don't owe me any apologies or explanations, and I trust you regardless. I DON'T trust that nigga though, and I promise you that he's absolutely bat shit crazy when it comes to you, so you have to be careful. The nigga is dangerous," I warned.

"I know that he can be obsessive, but I think saying that he's dangerous is giving him too much credit."

I looked at her for a few moments, trying to gauge rather or not she was truly ready to hear the ugly truth about the nigga she'd been playing house with. I knew that it would depend on how deep into the abusive cycle she was with him as to whether or not she was lying to herself about what Roland was capable of. Despite how good things were going with her and I, I knew that my words might not be enough to convince her about him without some type of smoking gun. Luckily for me, I'd seen this moment coming, and I was ready to bring her straight facts from a trusted source.

"I respect your opinion, bae, but I need you to keep an open mind and consider the possibility that I might not know more than you; I might just know DIFFERENT," I said.

This time, it was her that went silent, and the way her eyes roamed my face told me that she was evaluating me and my statement in a new light.

Before she could voice whatever was cycling through her beautiful mind, I saw Stoney's ears perk up as her head swung in the direction of the front door. Seconds later, the doorbell chimed melodically, and Stoney was moving at top speed in the direction of our guest.

"Are you expecting someone, David?"

"Yeah, and I need you to keep your emotions in check once this conversation gets going. No matter WHAT, I need you to maintain your composure. Agreed?"

She hesitated for a few seconds, looking in the direction Stoney had gone in before looking back to me.

"Who's here, David?"

"Answer the question that I asked you first," I insisted.

"Okay, I agree to TRY and keep my shit together. Now, who the hell is at the door?"

"Go answer it," I replied, sitting back comfortably on the couch.

Her look was a hybrid between suspicion and skepticism, but her curiosity forced her up and toward the front door. A few moments later, I heard voices, followed by nervous laughter, and then Stoney came bolting back around the corner, headed straight for me like she was being chased. I thought she wanted to play, but the way her body was shaking gave me a hint that something was wrong. When Ty came back around the corner, I was scratching Stoney behind the ears while whispering to her, which had a calming effect, but the moment she spotted Tesha, her body tensed up again.

"You got my dog confused as hell right now, and she doesn't like it," Ty said, sitting beside me on the couch and taking Stoney from me.

These actions signaled to Stoney who her mommy was, and she curled up right beside Tynesha, relaxed and content.

"Your dog, huh?" I asked, watching them with slight envy.

"Stay focused, David, and explain to me why my sister is here... or you can explain for yourself, Tesha," Ty offered.

She looked calm and patient outwardly, but I could hear something different in her voice, and it sounded like suspicion.

"D, can I use your bathroom first?" Tesha asked.

"First door on your right," Ty replied for me.

As soon as Tesha left the room, I felt the heat from Ty openly staring at me, but there was no hostility. YET.

"Why is Tesha here?"

"Just be patient, bae, and she's gonna explain everything that I can't," I replied calmly.

"Yeah, well, she better come the fuck on because I DON'T like surprises any-muthafuckin-way."

I accepted her comments without reacting with the smart ass retort I was thinking and busied myself by going to the kitchen to get something to drink. A bottle of water had been my intended target, but instead, I grabbed the bottle of Branson Cognac sitting on the kitchen counter. No shot glass was required. I simply unscrewed the top, turned it upside down, and let the smooth amber rocket fuel coat my mouth and throat.

I took two healthy swigs before returning back to the living room. When I got there, Tesha was sitting in the spot I'd vacated, and poor Stoney was almost completely in Tynesha's lap. As hazardous as it was to my health and my life expectancy, I still chose to sit in between the two women. You best believe that I was praying my ass off though.

"What was so urgent that I had to come out at this time of night, D?" Tesha asked.

"So, you invited her?" Ty asked.

"Yeah, I texted her to swing through when I was on my way here, and Tesha, it's important because I need Ty to fully understand the danger. Right now, she still thinks shit is sweet with this nigga, Roland."

"I never said that shit was sweet, David. I just don't got that nigga, Roland, being as dangerous as you're trying to say he is. The niggas he runs with might be some certified hittas, but he's just a crooked cop trying to get ahead," Ty stated.

"You have NO IDEA who Roland really is, Tynesha," Tesha said sarcastically.

"Oh, and you do?" Ty asked, looking past me to her sister.

"I know EXACTLY who Roland Simms is," Tesha said calmly.

I could tell that Ty wasn't really paying attention to the shit Tesha was saying, but as the silence got thicker between them two, I saw uncertainty creep over Ty's facial features. I didn't intend for this to turn into some ratchet shit between sisters, so I was prepared to play peacekeeper.

"Tesha, I need you to tell her what she DOESN'T know about ole boy, and Tynesha, I need you to listen," I said.

"Why? What good is it gonna do?" Tesha asked.

"It has to be done because we all have to be on the same page. There's no turning back now," I replied.

"What does that mean?" Tesha asked warily.

"What the fuck is going on with you two?" Ty asked suddenly.

When my eyes snapped to her face, I had to quickly remind myself that she couldn't possibly be talking about me and Tesha fucking, and then, I was allowed to breathe again.

"Tell her, Tesha," I prompted while still looking at Ty.

I heard Tesha let out an exaggerated sigh of obvious frustration behind me, but then, she started to speak the truth that needed telling. I watched the picture show of emotions contort and morph across Tynesha's face as she listened in disbelief, and my heart actually hurt for her because she now knew the lies that had been her life for almost two solid years. When Tesha stopped talking, Ty asked her a few questions, and then, they both fell silent.

"Okay, David, it's your turn to explain. Why did she need to know exactly who the devil is NOW as opposed to never?" Tesha asked.

"Because I just pulled the devil's tail, and he's sure to bite me for it," I replied.

"Pulled it how?" Ty asked.

I hesitated while trying to choose my words carefully, but I quickly realized that there was no nice way to make the ugly truth pretty.

"I killed his nephew, Q."

"What?!" Both women replied in unison.

"I ran down on him, pressed him for a little info, and then I sent him on to the afterlife as an act of mercy."

"Roland is gonna come at you with EVERYTHING he's got, you fool ass nigga!" Tesha said angrily.

"Or he's gonna make sure that you get thrown beneath the worst prison in the state of Florida," Ty chimed in, shaking her head in disgust.

"He's not gonna do any of that because he's gonna be too busy looking over his shoulder," I replied, smiling.

"What the fuck are you talking about?" Tesha asked.

"I'd be a damn fool to make one offensive move and then switch to playing only defense. Nah, I'm playing ALL offense until it benefits me to play defense, so that means I keep attacking him strategically," I replied.

"You mean killing more people," Ty said with obvious disapproval.

"Only if I have to," I vowed.

"Oh, you DEFINITELY have to now that you've started, you jackass, so please tell me that you have a plan," Tesha said.

"Wait, hold the fuck up. Tesha, you're actually agreeing to get involved in this crazy ass shit?" Ty asked in disbelief.

"Sis, were you NOT listening? I've BEEN involved in this crazy ass shit! I just want my life back at this point, so you damn right I'ma ride with David to kill Goliath," Tesha said emphatically.

The look of being overwhelmed was spreading across Ty's face faster than ice cracking under some serious weight, but I knew that she could handle it.

"No more lies or lies by omission, which means that we ALL stay on the same page, and none of this surprise shit like what just happened. We're in this together," Ty said.

"Do we explain any of this to Mom?" Tesha asked.

"Hell nah! She can't know nothing about Roland because she'll get dumb on that nigga, and she'll beat your muthafuckin ass for being out here in these streets. This is one secret that you better die with," Ty advised.

I nodded in agreement while locking eyes with Tesha and silently communicating that ALL secrets were going with us to the grave. Period.

"So, what's your plan, D?" Tesha asked.

"We're gonna rob, Roland," I replied simply.

"Huh?" Ty asked, holding her hand by her ear as if she didn't hear me.

"Are you talking about money, product, or both?" Tesha asked seriously.

"Q said that Roland doesn't handle product like that, but he keeps his hands in the money."

"You believe him?" Ty asked.

"It wasn't the right time to lie, so I think he told me nothing but the truth."

"From what I know, Roland don't fuck with the work because my shit always dropped off by different Lyft drivers.

He collects the money from me on Saturday, and I typically ride around the city with him to do the rest of the money grabs."

"Why?" Ty asked with hints of jealously peppering the air around that question.

"I don't know, maybe just for the purposes of being arm candy. He spends money on me while I'm with him, and he always gives me a few extra dollars once the pickups are done, and the money is counted. I guess I'm like his unofficial secretary," Tesha replied.

"Sounds cozy. Tell me, did you suck his dick and cook dinner for him too?" Ty asked half-jokingly.

"What did you say?" Tesha asked softly.

Her voice sounded calm and oh so innocent to the casual observer, but the edge was right there below the surface, sharper than Japanese steel.

"Chill out, baby," I said, shaking my head.

"Nah, David, I think it's a fair question to ask my beloved TWIN since she's so eager to speak about her secret life as a dope boy's assistant. All your LIFE, you wanted to be an assistant pimp," Ty said, laughing maliciously.

"Baby, I'm cool with being a worker because I'm earning my spot through blood, sweat, and tears like a real one should. You earned your position through CUM, sweat, and tears, and you better than me at that because I would NEVER," Tesha said, smiling with just as much malice as Ty was pushing at her.

I could feel this situation about to spiral out of control with the quickness, and that was the last thing I needed.

"Ayo, are you two really sitting here throwing shade at each other over a pure fuck nigga? You are two of the baddest bitches walking the PLANET so tell me how the fuck this shit makes sense right now! Tynesha, that nigga tried to break you mentally, emotionally, and physically, so where he puts his dick or spends his time shouldn't even fucking matter. And Tesha, this same lame nigga has been fucking you every way except for physically because you're his goddamn SLAVE! He might as well put the money on the nightstand in your case because that's what he's using to control you. Put your lives into perspective and then listen to how incredibly STUPID you both sound right now. Tighten the fuck up," I said, standing up and heading for the front door.

When I stooped down to pick up Stoney's leash, it got her attention, and she came running toward me. I hooked the leash on her, grabbed a few shit bags, and lit a pre-rolled blunt before walking out of the condo. Even though I was walking aimlessly, I still made sure to pay attention to my surroundings, which was why I spotted the cops staking out my spot as my feet hit the sidewalk. I wasn't surprised that I was being watched, but I could tell that a middle of the night pop out by me had caught them flat footed because they had no natural moves to make inside their unmarked Jeep Grand Cherokee. It was two, middle aged, white men that would blend in seamlessly with daytime foot traffic in this area but sitting together in the Jeep at this moment SCREAMED law enforcement. The ignorant part of me wanted to walk straight up on their ride and knock on the window, but instead, I took a lap around the block, puffing thoughtfully on my blunt. By the time I got back in front of my building, the blunt was gone, Stoney had done her business, and I had a wild idea of how to set shit off. I ran upstairs and let myself in, expecting to see two grown ass women sitting on opposite ends of the couch, pouting, but instead, I opened the door to the smell of bacon cooking. Stoney and I went to the kitchen where we found Tynesha and Tesha working together, whipping up a delicious smelling brunch while the sounds of Mary J. Blige played from my hidden speakers.

"I've got an idea," I announced.

Neither woman said anything or even looked in my direction, but I knew damn well that they heard me.

"Siri, pause music selection," I commanded.

Sudden silence filled the kitchen, and that made both women turn to face me.

"I've got an idea," I said again.

"I'm sure you do, but it'll have to wait until we execute our plan," Ty said.

"What plan?" I asked.

The smile that they both gave me was identical in beauty and mischievousness, and it gave me the chills.

Chapter 11

"What plan?" I asked again, looking back-and-forth between them.

Tesha glanced at Ty, and once she got the nod from her, she moved over toward me.

"Since Ty and I only have our own individual experiences to draw from, we thought it would help to see life through each other's eyes."

I looked at Tesha for a second, and once I realized that she was serious, I looked over at Ty.

"Are you two talking about some trading places type shit?" I asked.

"Yeah, but..."

"Stop. Do you think this is some type of muthadfuckin movie or something?! I guarantee you that this nigga got real bullets in his gun, so what do you think he's gonna do when he finds out that you two simple ass think that this is a game?" I asked, shaking with frustration coursing through my body.

"D, he's not gonna find out, so why are you tripping?" Ty asked, coming to stand next to her sister.

My anger was building swiftly, like a wildfire in the middle of a field full of dried grass, and their look of calm determination was like adding the blowing wind to the equation. After everything that we'd discussed, I'd thought that they both understood the severity of the situation and just how dangerous this all was, but I was wrong. These bitches were trippin!

"I'm gonna say this one more time, and I need you both to listen to me like your life depends on it. There's no way I'm going along with you two switching identities just for the fuck of it because it's not worth the risk. I just told you that I killed this nigga's favorite nephew, and there ain't no coming back from that. So, let's say he does discover the switch that you two pulled off, Do you really think that he's not gonna automatically suspect everything that you have done or could've done? I'm telling you this muthafucka is liable to kill you simply because he doesn't trust anyone around him anymore, so now ain't the time for weird shit. Every move we make has to make sense three moves from now because that's the only way to stay ahead of him," I said sincerely.

My words once again caused them to look at each other in silent communication, which made me feel like I was getting through to them somewhat. I understood them wanting to help and actively participate, but there was no room for even the slightest mistakes - not unless they wanted to end up as a story on the ten o'clock news.

"So, what was your brilliant idea, David?" Ty asked.

"It's simple really. I think we should align ourselves with Roland's opps," I replied.

"That's crazy because we actually entertained that same idea for a whole thirty seconds before we found the fatal flaw in that plan," Tesha said.

"Take your time though," Ty added, smiling sarcastically.

I felt myself readying my tongue to unleash a torrent of blistering words that resonated from my soul, but I somehow maintained my composure - for the moment at least.

"Why don't you explain to me why the enemy of my enemy isn't my friend?" I replied calmly.

"Ultimately, no one is gonna trust you enough to go to war with the cops or the Haitians for you. You might have a couple of toes in these waters, but at the end of the day, we're talking about big business, and niggas will kill all of us before we're allowed to stand in the way of that," Tesha stated.

"The evil they know will always be preferred to the evil they don't," Ty surmised logically.

Even though I wanted to argue with their words, I couldn't because their logic was making too much sense for a smart person to ignore. Roland wasn't a problem that was going to get fixed overnight, not even if I put a bullet through his diabolical brain. I could admit to myself that I was feeling a certain sense of pressure to solve this problem as soon as possible because I felt exposed and vulnerable, and I detested those feelings. It was one thing to get into it with a street nigga who had some muscle behind him, but this situation was all types of worse. There was no way for me to get on a level playing field with this nigga because he was the cheat code himself! I had to move different different.

"What are you thinking, D?" Tesha asked.

"That this shit feels like mission impossible," I replied, grinding my back teeth in a nervous habit.

"He's not untouchable, and neither are the niggas he's running with. What's your plan for turning his friends against him?" Ty asked.

"By robbing him, I make him a liability instead of an asset, which is why I suggested it," I replied.

"Yeah, but is one robbery enough to turn the tide?" Tesha asked skeptically.

"That's why we hit multiple targets and do the most damage possible," I stated.

"You mean hit everyone he picks up from?" Tesha asked.

"Exactly, and I know that you know who they are. All I need you to do is give me the list of names and locations, and I got it from there," I assured her.

"Or you can let us help you," Ty said softly.

"What?" Tesha and I asked in unison, looking at Tynesha for an explanation.

"Your goal is to turn Roland's allies against him, which means that you have to give them a believable lie to run with. They might believe that Roland was incompetent enough to get robbed, but you run a bigger risk that they'll just chalk it up as part of the game. But... if the woman who is always with Roland is the one laying niggas down, then it looks like either Roland put her up to it or he's too tender dick to be of use to Zoe Pound anymore. If we really wanna sell the dream, then Tesha and I pull the heist together because there's no way that anyone would believe that Roland's personal life and business life went rogue together," Ty said, smirking.

I looked back-and-forth between Tynesha and Tesha, and I caught Tesha looking back-and-forth between Ty and me. Based on Tesha's facial expression, I knew that her and I had to be thinking the same thing.

"Ty, how did your square ass put together the ultimate triple cross when you don't even be in the streets like that?" I asked, genuinely impressed.

"My sweet David, how quickly you forget that warfare isn't limited to the streets, and muthafuckas have been planning coupés while secured behind castle walls for years. More importantly though, you forget that women are the deadliest assassins in the world because the thought of good pussy disarms a man. Trust me when I tell you that Roland's people know that the nigga is good and whipped when it comes to my fine red ass, so they'll have no problem imagining what he'd do for the prospect of having me and Tesha as his."

"I gotta admit, sis, this is well played, and it'll definitely work. I didn't think that you had it in you, bitch, but I guess that I'm not the only one like our parents," Tesha said.

They shared a look that I didn't understand, but it was over too quick for me to ask about it in a natural way. Right now, I needed to focus on what was in front of me so that it didn't sneak up behind me.

"Okay, so how do we do this?" I asked, looking directly at Tesha.

"Let's discuss it over breakfast," Ty suggested, going back to the stove.

By 3 a.m., we were sitting around my dining room table, putting together the intricate details necessary to pull this shit off. For the most part, Tesha said a lot of the niggas who were holding would give it up smooth when the gun was put in their faces, but there were a few who would require violent persuasion. We agreed to start with the hardheaded muthafuckas first since killing them was a probability and not merely a possibility, but it would also serve to warn anyone else who thought to refuse. Play with someone else because we were so serious. The number of people that we had to hit was twelve total, and since it was already Saturday, the odds were good when it came to whether or not the money was ready for pickup. Tesha was able to give us a blueprint so that we knew what type of currency to expect because not everyone dealt in cash. Cryptocurrency and gold were involved, but I didn't mind because diversifying my portfolio was one of the goals of my scamming. I was always looking for ways to improve my wealth while sustaining its invisibility because I wasn't the loud type. I didn't need to look like a millionaire because that brought endless questions that would only complicate the simple lies I'd told thus far. No one in the world would believe that I currently had fourteen million dollars scattered around the world in the form of assets, artwork, and even a vintage wine collection. That was exactly how I wanted it though. This lick we were about to pull off would add nicely to my quiet empire, and the knowledge of this made me smile to myself.

"You like this shit, don't you?" Tesha asked suddenly.

"Huh?" I replied, wondering what I'd missed.

"I said that you like this shit, and I can tell because of the light in your eyes. Here I thought that you were quiet, sweet, David Bishop, who made good grades and respected women, but the whole time you've been with the shit," Tesha said, shaking her head while chuckling lightly.

"I'm still respectful of women," I replied, smiling at Ty.

"Of course you are... but there's so much more to you than meets the eye, Mr. Bishop," Tesha stated as if she was suddenly privy to secrets of my keeping.

The look of humor didn't shift in Tynesha's eyes, but Tesha's comments made me self-conscious about certain secrets coming to light, so I quickly shifted the focus back to safer topics. "Ty, are you sure that you're comfortable reaching out to Roland?" I asked.

"You've asked me that three times already, and I've promised you that I'm good. I'm gonna have him meet me for breakfast, kick it long enough to establish an alibi, and then sneak off to link up with you and Tesha."

"I'll be watching everything through Dunkin Donuts live security footage, and when the time comes, that same footage will be provided to Zoe Pound. It's gonna look like you took a meeting with Roland, heard the plans, and then did what you were told," I said.

"A picture is worth a thousand words, but a video is priceless," Tesha said, smiling widely.

"Listen, pulling this shit off is the easy part compared to what happens next," I warned.

"What do you mean?" Ty asked.

"I mean, once this is done, your lives will forever be changed, and ain't no going back. You need to think about that before it's too late," I advised.

Tynesha and Tesha looked at each other and communicated in that way that was beyond my understanding. I knew that we would all agree that it was necessary to get rid of Roland, so the only question was if this plan was the best one.

"I'm in this with you, bitch," Tesha vowed.

"And I'd never leave you for dead, hoe," Ty replied.

"So then it's settled," I said, standing up and heading for my bedroom closet.

I knelt in front of the safe that set immediately inside the walk-in closet to the right of the door, but what I wanted was in the shoe box beside the safe. I reached inside and grabbed the extra key fob to my BMW, and then, I returned to the dining room. When I sat back down at the table, all eyes were on me, but I simply slid the key fob to Tynesha and picked my fork back up.

"Awww, does this make you two official?" Tesha asked sarcastically.

I didn't respond. My eyes just stayed locked on Ty's face. I saw her finger immediately go to the panic button on the key fob, which was the only feature that made it different from the one on my key ring sitting in the bowl by the front door.

"What happens when I press this?" Ty asked, glancing up at me curiously.

"You're mine... forever," I replied.

Her eyes filled with intrigue and nothing close to fear, which was what I expected.

"How the hell is a key fob gonna join you two forever?" Tesha asked in obvious disbelief.

I still didn't pay her any attention though. I was locked in on Ty to see what she would do next. As the seconds passed, I could feel and see her curiosity grow until she finally pressed the square red button. She immediately flinched, but she didn't drop the key fob as blood oozed from the pin hole prick in her thumb.

"Wh-what was that?" Ty asked, still staring at me.

"Bitch, are you bleeding?" Tesha asked, reaching for her sister's hand.

Ty moved her hand out of Tesha's reach, but her attention was on me, awaiting my answer.

"Your DNA is part of my security protocol now, meaning you have access to all the things that I own that are restricted to everyone else," I replied.

"Bullshit. Are you some type of super spy now, my nigga?" Tesha asked, laughing.

Ty and I continued to stare at each other for a few seconds, and then, she started looking around the condo like she was seeing it for the first time.

"Does this have anything to do with the timer I saw on the bathroom mirror when I took a shower the other day?" Ty asked.

"What?" Tesha asked, confused.

"It does," I replied, smiling.

"You two are weird as fuck but whatever. Can we just get back to the task at hand?" Tesha said impatiently.

"We need guns," Ty said, raising an eyebrow at me.

"You're right. We do. Go get a few," I replied, sitting back in my seat and paying attention to my food.

"You want her to go pick up some guns by herself, D? You must be high, my nigga," Tesha said.

"Chill out, T. I think I understand, and I don't gotta go far," Ty said, standing up and heading toward the bathroom. I heard the bathroom door close, and then, the sounds of water running could be heard coming from behind that door.

"Either you're smoking something or you need to smoke something, David. I'm just gonna need you to figure it out and stop acting crazy. I know what it really is. You just need some more of this good pussy," Tesha said in a loud whisper.

"Ayo, chill the fuck out with that shit before Ty hears you," I snapped, giving her a threatening look.

Her normally beautiful smile was contorted by the deviousness entwined with her spirit, and I knew that I was partially to blame. I couldn't change that because what was done was done, but she better know that the moment I felt threatened by our secret, I wouldn't hesitate to make her disappear. I heard the water shut off, which told me that time was running out with regards to privacy.

"Don't say or do shit to make your sister suspicious and I'm not playing about that," I said.

The sound of the bathroom door opening froze Tesha's comments, but the shit eating grin on her face said more than words. When she saw what was in Ty's hand, her smile faltered, but Ty's was as radiant as ever.

"What the fuck is that, and where did you get it?" Tesha asked.

"It's a Sig Sauer P290 Carbine .223, which is an automatic handgun that shoots AK-47 rounds faster than a chopper can," I replied.

"David... that's yours?!" Tesha asked in disbelief.

"It's one of his," Ty said, looking at me with more curiosity than before.

"What's mine is yours now," I said, giving a slight nod toward her finger that she'd bled from.

I knew that she understood, in part because her palm had been scanned on the bathroom mirror in order for her to gain access to the gun in her hand or the secret compartments that held the rest. It was deeper than that though, but further explanation would have to wait until later.

"We've got the plan, and we've got the guns. So, what's next?" Tesha asked.

"Someone has to tell Mommy because she has to be moved to safety," Ty said.

Both women looked at each other before their eyes finally swung in my direction, and I instantly had a stomach bubbling bad feeling.

"David, you know that I like you a lot, right?" Ty asked sweetly.

Tesha was chuckling, but I was already squirming. I'd prefer shooting someone than facing the wrath of their mother.

"You two owe me," I said, addressing both of them by pointing my fingers.

"And I'll pay you," Ty said.

"Gladly," Tesha chimed in.

Chapter 12

I knew that I had a few hours before the sun took back to the sky like it had unfinished business, so using the remaining darkness to my advantage was the reason I opted to go get Tonya immediately. I had no idea how she was about to respond to my demands that she leave her home, but hopefully, me coming in the names of her daughters was enough to persuade her. At first, I'd thought that bringing Tonya to my condo was the safe move, but during my drive across town, I'd realized that putting us all under the same roof made for one stop shopping when it came to killing us. Tonya needed to be separated and kept off the radar. In an effort to be more inconspicuous, I'd elected to drive the navy blue, 2024 Dodge Challenger Hellcat Redeye that no one knew I owned in order to scoop Tonya up. The car was registered to a shell company that was connected by another shell company, which couldn't be traced back to me, no matter how hard someone tried. The secret apartment that I planned to hide Tonya in was under the same fictitious names for mailing purposes, thereby making it undetectable and safe for the time being. At a quarter to 4 a.m., I pulled up on Tonya's block and went to the front door instead of around the back like I had a few days before now. It took a long time for Tonya to respond to my beating on her door on some hostile shit, and when she did, you could see clearly that she was big mad.

"David? What the fuck are you doing here?" she asked, looking behind me over my shoulders.

"There's a situation, and I need you to come with me, and we don't have a lot of time."

"We've got enough time for you to explain your damn self," she replied, folding her arms across her sizable chest and leaning against the door jam.

The way her silk negligée hugged her athletic build made it hard to concentrate on her face, even though I doubted that she could see my eyes curiously roaming in the darkness.

"You're in danger, and we gotta go," I said, moving past her into the house.

"Danger? What do you mean, and where the hell are my kids, David?"

"They're safe, and they sent me to get you," I replied.

"Why would they send you to get me?"

"That's a dumb ass question, but obviously because they love you, and they don't want you to die just yet. Now, I need you to pack a bag so that we can get the fuck out of here," I stated firmly.

When I looked back at her over my shoulder, I saw the numerous questions that she wanted to ask me, but the exasperation on my face deterred further commentary.

"Wait here. It'll only take me a minute," she said, closing the front door behind us and heading toward the back of the house.

While I waited, I sent a message to Tynesha to let her know that I'd made it here, and we'd be on the move soon if I could keep from killing her mom my damn self. I didn't bother telling her exactly where I was taking her mom because that was a face-to-face conversation we would have at the right time. Right now, I didn't know if anyone was intercepting or monitoring our messages, so playing it safe was the only way to go. As the minutes ticked by, I could feel the anxiety in the pit of my stomach growing until the tightness in my bowels became more than an irritant. I was just about to find the nearest bathroom when Tonya suddenly reappeared, wearing a black, Nike, sweatsuit and carrying a matching black, mini, duffle bag.

"I'm ready if you are," she said, attempting to hand me the bag.

"Oh, I'm ready, but we put our own work in around here, so you can hold onto you bag."

Her irritation flashed briefly across her beautiful face for a second in a way that reminded me of her daughters, but it vanished just as quick. It was replaced by a look of sudden terror.

"Did you hear that?" she asked in a fierce whisper, moving close enough to me for me to smell the scent of Jasmine on her skin.

"I heard something, but..."

I'd just been about to tell her not to worry because it was nothing when I saw the silhouette of someone creeping right outside of her living room window. The rational side of me said that this couldn't possibly be anyone dangerous because their movements were too brazen, but at four o'clock in the morning, it wasn't rationality that I was listening to. My instincts had me reaching for the Taurus G3C 9mm pistol at the small of my back, raising it to shoulder height on the still moving shadow outside the window, and tapping the trigger twice like it was a PlayStation game controller. Glass exploded with the booming sounds of gunshots, and whoever had decided to walk amongst Tonya's rose bushes hit the ground to forever push up daisies. Had it been a mistake on my part then the night would've fallen silent after my shots, but instead, a beautiful symphony ensued. Before I heard the deep throated bellow of bullets serenading me, I saw at least three barrels glowing in the dark a few feet away, and I knew which direction to avoid moving. I barely had time to grab Tonya and push her to safety before bullets came fast, flying into the house. I fired back blindly, remembering in my mind's eye which direction I'd seen the shots coming from as I tried to keep us both from getting hit. My car was parked halfway up the block out front of her house, but the only way that we were going to get there was taking the long way around.

"Come on and stay low," I demanded, pulling Tonya toward Tesha's bedroom.

The sound of gunshots was still loud as we crept toward the back of the house, but the rhythm changed, and I knew that meant someone either had a switch on their Glock or something firing automatic had joined the party. Either way, I didn't want to get hit, so I kept scrambling low like I was trying to get to the bottom of a dog pile and recover the fumbled football. As soon as we made it to Tesha's room, I stood up straight and ran for the window that led us outside. The darkness surrounding us inside the room allowed for my eyes to adjust to the moonlit night with minimum effort, so I immediately spotted the two niggas creeping toward the back door of the house with their guns outstretched in front of them. I waited for them to move past Tesha's darkened window before I lifted it just enough to be able to shoot out of. The ringing of gunfire that echoed from the front to the back of the house covered up the three shots that I let off in quick succession and masked the thud of the two dead bodies hitting the dew-covered grass when they dropped.

"Follow me and stay close," I ordered, pushing the window all the way up so that we could climb out.

When I looked back, Tonya had her bag slung over her shoulder and around her neck, and she was clutching a dangerous looking chrome .38 snub nose pistol with the wood handle in her left hand. Hopefully, she knew how to use the muthafucka, and she wouldn't accidentally put a bullet in the back of my skull. Once my feet hit the ground, I took off at a dead sprint, making a beeline for the neighbor's yard. I could feel Tonya right on my heels, so I didn't bother to pause and catch my breath. I just kept running like my name ended in Gump, and bullets were biting. We hopped the fence and then skirted the corner of the next house over, which put us far enough away for the gunshots to sound faint and sporadic. I used the keyless remote in my pocket to start my car, and once I didn't see armed goons descend on my ride, I quickly led the way from the shadows. I didn't even have the door closed all the way before I had the car in gear and was pulling off at a slow creep, heading away from Tonya's house. Part of me wanted to put all my weight on the gas pedal, but that would draw attention to my car, and then, the element of surprise was forfeited for this vehicle and anything attached to it. The shooting continued even as I put distance between us and the bullets, and I felt my adrenaline begin to dissipate a little. My nerves followed, and within minutes, I could no longer taste the fear on my tongue, only the anger. The farther I drove, the angrier I got, and by the time we'd taken the emergency scenic route that ended with us parked in front of my apartment building, I was emotionally wrapped in the cold fury that always predicted someone's death. The only thing that I had left to figure out was who was going to die.

"Tonya, listen to me carefully. I want you to go into apartment 1b using the ground floor side entrance, lock the door, and don't open it for any reason. I'm the only one who can get into that apartment besides Tynesha, and she doesn't know that it exists yet. You'll be safe as long as you do exactly what I tell you."

"But, David, what the hell is going on, and who is shooting at you?"

"Shooting at me? Them niggas wasn't there shooting at me. They were coming for you and Tesha," I stated matter-of-factly.

"That's bullshit because don't nobody have a reason to want me or Tesha dead. None of this crazy shit started happening until you came into the picture, which means it's you they want."

"Look, you have no fucking clue what's going on so just keep your opinions to yourself and talk to me nicely for saving your life. Now, get out of my damn car and go inside," I replied dismissively.

The look I gave her was one of expectancy for her to follow instructions, but she sat stuck in my front seat with her mouth hanging open wide enough for her chin to meet her chest.

"You need me to slow it down for you or pull you out of the car?" I asked, putting the car in park just in case.

"I-I'm going. It's just you-you're different. The way you're talking to me is completely different from who I thought you were."

"Whatever. Just get out so that I can get back to Ty and Tesha," I said.

"Don't you think it makes sense for you to actually check out the apartment before you leave me? I mean, I know you say that no one knows about this spot, but I think you would agree that it's better to be safe than sorry."

Even knowing that she was right didn't change my feelings of wanting to punch her teeth up into her gums for the hell of it. Only the moral fact that hitting or beating women was wrong kept me from doing her dirty like a nigga in the street, but I was still pissed off.

"Man, bring your ass in here," I said, shutting the car off and climbing out.

My pistol was on my side, concealed by my shirt, because I didn't want to draw attention to myself by walking with the gun out. I remained highly vigilant as I led the way into the building and down one flight of steps, but there was nothing that seemed out of the ordinary. The apartment building itself was a nondescript high rise in the heart of downtown Orlando, but what made it special was its security features. It was built like a bank vault, and no one could gain entry without a coded keycard that was set to the biometrics of the owner of the apartment. You couldn't rent an apartment here;

you could only own one, and in order to do that, you had to be sponsored by a family member on the housing committee. The committee was comprised of diplomats from different countries, which made the entire high rise and the land it set on untouchable by U.S. government forces. The best part was that only the people who needed to know about this building's existence were the ones who knew, so what happened inside these walls wasn't open to public scrutiny. This was the devil's playground, and demon time was what ensued once you entered. I used the chip imbedded in my right wrist to gain entry to the first floor from the stairway and then again to gain access into my apartment itself.

The spare key that I'd given Tonya would've been just as effective when it came to gaining access, but as a stranger, she would've been surveilled by everyone in the building. There was complete privacy in each of the apartments of course, but there were literally cameras everywhere else, and they watched everything and everyone who wanted part of this 'family' of ours. I'd inherited the two apartments that I owned in this building from the father I could barely remember, and being here had saved my life before, so this was the safest place I knew on Earth. There were eighteen floors with two apartments on each floor that rivalled the size of any New York penthouse on the Hudson River. There was more than enough room for me, Ty, Tesha, and Tonya under the same roof, but I was smart enough not to trap us all in close proximity. Tesha would be here with her mom, and Ty would stay with me in my apartment on the twelfth floor. I did a quick walkthrough and check of the four bedrooms, two bathrooms, computer room, and my private library before returning to the living room where I found Tonya sitting on the couch, preoccupied with her phone.

"You're good. No one is here except for you so keep the door locked, and we'll be back soon."

"Who is we?" she asked.

"I'm bringing Tesha here to stay with you, and Tynesha will stay with me at another spot I've got off the grid," I replied impatiently.

"I think it'll be better for all of us to be under the same roof, so you and Ty can just stay here too."

"No thanks," I replied, heading for the front door.

"You're misunderstanding me, David, because I wasn't asking you. I'm telling you what you're gonna do."

Ordinarily, I would've laughed at anyone telling me what I was going to do because that position of authority was tentatively held by God. Something in Tonya's tone made me stop and look back though. The smirk on her face was one derived from self-satisfaction, but on this woman's face, there was danger in the beauty. My instincts had told me that.

"Why would you ever think that I'd listen to you?" I asked curiously.

The smirk on her face increased in width as she turned her phone to face me. At first, I thought that she was showing me her porn preferences because there was a man and a woman fucking on her phone's screen, but then, the man switched positions, and my breathing stopped.

"You'll listen to me because deep down I know you love Tynesha... Even though you're currently dick deep inside Tesha on this video. Just out of curiosity, David, who's better in bed?"

My hand was itching for the gun on my hip to jump into my palm and scratch it by putting a few bullets in her smile. It would solve my immediate problem, but it would potentially create a bigger one that no amount of damage control would fix. Finesse was sorely needed, along with the patience of God. I had a lot of questions running laps around my tongue, competing to see who the first off of pit road would be, but only one question and answer mattered at this exact moment.

"What do you want?" I asked, turning to face her completely.

"My dear, David, all I want is equality. Nothing more, nothing less."

"Cryptic shit will get you shot right now, so why don't you just tell me how much equality is gonna cost so that I can be on my way?" I said, knowing that if her number was disrespectfully high, then I was putting a bullet between her eyes asap.

"Your money is no good here," she replied, putting her phone into her sweatpant's pocket.

Before I could seek further clarification on payment options or her terms, she casually pushed her sweatpants to the floor while taking off her sweatshirt. No bra cradled her succulent breasts, and there wasn't a stitch of fabric to guard her most sacred of secrets. One thing was absolutely clear though, and that was the origin of the gorgeous bodies that Tynesha and Tesha were known for. They ab-so-lutely got it from their mama!

"Lord, help me," I mumbled, shaking my head as Tonya came closer toward me.

I was a firm believer that God heard all prayers, but it quickly became clear to me that there was a waiting list and a line before you got an answer to those prayers. I was on my own for the moment, truly about to become one with the devil in her playground.

Chapter 13

"What took you so long to get back? You had me worried," Tynesha said, pulling the door open before I could put my key in the lock.

"I had to make sure that your mom was safe and calm her down because her nerves were a hot ass mess. Are you two ready to go?"

"Go where? Shit, this might be the safest place in the city," Tesha said from her seat at my dining room table.

I closed the front door and motioned for Ty to follow me so that I wouldn't have to repeat myself. Stoney kept running into my legs on purpose, trying to get my attention and play, but I ignored her because I had bigger hands to hold through this crisis.

"The safest place in the city is my other apartment where I stashed your mom at. We're gonna hit this lick and then hold up there while Roland tries to stop the bleeding," I said.

"Why wouldn't he just come to your other spot to get you or us? I mean, the fact that him and his people just shot up my mom's shit should tell you that nothing is off limits, and nowhere is safe," Ty said.

"And you still wanna rob this nigga?" Tesha asked in slight disbelief.

"You gotta trust me when I tell you that we'll be safe there, but I'll explain later when we have more time. And you muthafuckin right. We still gonna rob this nigga! We already got him making impulsive decisions based off of emotions because there was no way he thought it through before going after your mom. What purpose would your mom's death serve besides causing you extreme pain? I doubt that it was even a retaliatory move for what I did to his nephew because it feels too personal. His nephew would've been looked at from a business perspective first because of the robbery that took place. That means I was just in the right place at the right time to save your mother, but it's evident that this nigga, Roland, is coming unglued," I concluded.

"So, we keep poking him?" Tesha asked.

"Yeah... we do," Ty replied, nodding toward me in understanding.

It looked like Tesha had some more to say, but she kept her mouth shut and picked up the twin Glock .17s sitting on the table in front of her.

"Put them in the bag by the couch with the other guns," Ty instructed.

While Tesha did that, I turned to Ty and pulled her into my arms.

"You smell good for a man who was recently running for his life," she said, hugging me tightly.

"I took a quick shower because I definitely smelled like the baby's diaper after dodging the big shit they were trying to air mail my way. I ain't been back past your mom's house, but I'm telling you, babe, that them niggas was shooting something big enough to knock out chunks of concrete from a building's foundation."

"I'm just glad they missed," she murmured against my chest, holding me tighter.

As badly as I wanted Tynesha in my arms every moment of everyday, the guilt that I felt was so intense that it forced me to take a step back after a couple of moments. When I looked down at her, I could see the confusion and slight hurt, but I quickly smoothed it over with a kiss on the forehead, and then, I whispered something into her ear. Instantly, her smile lit up the room, and her hands dropped down to my ass where she gave me a gentle squeeze.

"You two can play grab ass later. Right now though, we need to go over the plan," Tesha said, coming back into the dining room.

I feigned reluctance at being interrupted even though inwardly I was only too happy to stay focused on business. I took a seat at the head of the table, which put Tesha on my left, and Ty took the seat on my right side.

"Alright, so the first spot we're gonna hit is run by a nigga named Taliban but don't let the name fool you because the nigga ain't built like them killers in the middle east. The nigga's real name is Jermaine, and he's a skinny kid originally from Richmond, Virginia. He's defined as a small-time hustler and full-time weird nigga by anyone who's spent more than five minutes around him. All he thinks about is getting his dick wet, and he doesn't discriminate between men and women when it comes to who wets his dick," Tesha said.

"So, is the play gonna be for you and I to approach, or do we just send David in with some skinny jeans on?" Ty asked, laughing.

"You got jokes," I said, not cracking a smile at the idea she presented.

Tesha laughed right along with her sister, but it was short lived once I turned my laser stare on her.

"Taliban is bisexual on paper. He prefers dick, but in order to keep up appearances, he stays with some bad bitches around him. Most of them are strung out on dope, so we're gonna have to blend in and act like customers to get through the front door. Then, we take control of the situation and let David in to take care of the business," Tesha explained.

"What makes you think that this nigga, Taliban, won't give it up?" I asked.

"He may be gay, and a whole bitch at heart, but he's an informant, and that makes him feel bulletproof. Him knowing that he can tell and basically get out of any trouble that comes his way has made him increasingly dangerous because he now thinks a muthafucka won't kill him. In his cognitive distortions, he believes that the streets actually respect and fear him. Having Roland on his team only made his attitude worse, which is why he needs killing," Tesha replied.

"How much is he holding?" I asked.

"A couple hundred grand in cash and probably the same amount in product depending on how bad he's stepped on it already. He's got a five-bedroom house that he shares with his little brother, Meiko, but there's really no telling how many people are in their house at any given time. Meiko is just like Taliban, except that his sexual preferences is minors, and he thinks that shit is cool," Tesha explained with an expression of utter disgust riding her facial features.

"So, there could be kids in this house?" Ty asked.

"Sadly, yeah. I mean, I've seen teenage girls running around the house and the outside property high off of fentanyl and not knowing what the fuck was going on. These niggas are predators, but my concern is someone dying that doesn't need to," Tesha confessed.

I weighed her words carefully as the picture that they painted manifested in my mind in three dimensions. I knew, and had known, that there would be collateral damage in the form of people dying that may not have anything to do with the ultimate goal. I was okay with that part, but this nigga, Taliban, presented a different issue that required real time analyzing. With all the unknowns that lurked behind the closed doors of his house, I had to mentally prepare for this shit to go very, very wrong. I knew that I could handle shit going bad because being indifferent was one of my superpowers, but Tynesha and Tesha weren't like me. They weren't broken inside, and I wasn't about to let them become broken because of me.

"Okay, so the way that we play this is you and Ty get me into the house, and then, I'll deal with whatever is inside while you two lead the women and children to safety. Understand?" I asked, looking back-and-forth between them.

They both nodded, and I could see the relief in their eyes now that they knew I was wearing the weight of any unforeseeable bad decisions coming our way.

"Alright, let's get started," I said, rising from my seat.

It took us about fifteen minutes to get the things that we needed and load up my Hellcat. I decided to leave my BMW parked, just to throw Roland off a little, but I really felt like it was time to get rid of it altogether. By 8 a.m., we were pulling up around the corner from Taliban's house, and we hopped out like three junkies trying to get well before going to work. Tesha and Ty knocked on the door while I stood just out of sight with the AR style shotgun pressed against my leg.

"Damn, girl, you and Roland are early today for pickup. You must be in need of a little pick me up too."

I didn't know Taliban to be able to recognize his voice but based on the words spoken by the man a few feet from me, I could surmise that this was our main target.

"We definitely came to party, Taliban. You alone?" Tesha asked nonchalantly.

"My little brother is downstairs sleeping it off, but it's just us and a few hoes. You two are some sho nuff steppas though so come on in and make yourself comfortable," he invited, a little too cheerfully.

Instead of stepping forward, Tesha took a step back, and Ty took a step to the side, which allowed me to swing around the corner with the 12 gauge out in front of me.

"Breathe slowly so that my trigger finger don't get nervous," I said, levelling the gun at his chin.

"Man, what the fuck is this?" Taliban asked, raising his hands with an annoyed look flooding his face.

"This is a robbery, my nigga, but homicide is on the menu if you'd like to order something to go," I replied, pressing my gun to his forehead and using it to push him backwards.

"How many upstairs; how many downstairs?" Tesha asked, pulling out her Glock .17 and chambering the first round by pulling the slide back swiftly.

"Two bitches and a nigga in my bedroom and whoever Meiko got down there with him. It don't matter though because you better kill us all if you're serious about your reason for being here. You must think I'm a bitch for real if you're gonna rob me and not kill me," Taliban remarked sarcastically.

"Of course you're a bitch, bruh, but that ain't the point. Tell me where everything is and this will be over before you know it," I assured him.

His response was to chuckle humorlessly, and then, the nigga did the most disrespectful thing imaginable. He spit in my face. Before the glob of mucus could slide in any direction on my forehead, I pulled the trigger and cleanly separated his head from his shoulders in a beautiful misting spray.

"You two go upstairs, and I'll take care of little brother," I said, wiping my face with my shirt as I moved.

The shotgun I was wielding had a built-in suppressor on it, but I still didn't think that there was any way my first shot had gone unheard. By the time I got to the bottom of the stairs, a bedroom door was opening, and a cute, blonde, white girl was peeking out. I would've brought into the idea of her succumbing to her curiosity, but her face was tearstained, and the fear in her eyes was one hundred percent authentic, which told me that there was more at play here.

"Ma'am, are you hurt?" I asked, using my best official sounding voice.

"We're good... I mean, I'm-I'm good. Is it safe to come out now?"

"Yeah, it's okay. The paramedics are upstairs with the rest of the cops," I said, bluffing.

"Cops," she said impulsively, giving me a look that symbolized distress.

Based on how she was standing in the doorway, I figured Meiko to be just over her left shoulder, out of sight and hidden by the shadows. With him being that close to her, there was no warning that could be given without detection, so I simply raised my gun and fired twice through the wall where I thought he was standing. Her scream was one of shock, and it was brief, but the sounds coming from the darkness that Meiko had considered safe were shades of agony harmonizing with regret, and it was beautiful music. The girl sprinted toward me, but I waved her up the stairs as I kept pushing toward my target. Meiko was down on the floor, cradling what was left of his right arm and crying like his mother's womb was the only real safety he'd ever known. I put the pump to the side of his head and pulled the trigger, which drilled his brains into the house's foundation like a termite infestation. A quick search of the room turned up some cash, a few guns, and a stash of porn with girls on the covers looking entirely too young for legal performance. I ignored everything but the money, and once I had that secured, I made my way back upstairs. I ran into Ty and Tesha, both dragging body bags full of something lucrative as evidenced by the huge grins plastered across their faces.

"We put the women in a bathroom, and I knocked the dude unconscious," Tesha said.

"Take the bags to the car and I'll meet you outside," I said, heading for the bedroom.

I checked on the women first, just to reassure them that they wouldn't be hurt as long as they forgot everything that had happened here, and then I collected everyone's information. On my way out, I put the 12 gauge to the base of the unconscious man's skull and pulled the trigger. The force of the shotgun blast knocked his forehead off and left it spinning around on the stained wooden floor in a strangely comical way. I kept my laughter to myself, looked around the house one more time, and then, I followed my codefendants' lead outside. By the time I made it to the car, Ty was in the driver's seat while Tesha leaned out the passenger side window with both pistols up and covering my back as I got in.

"Well, that went smoothly," I said facetiously.

"I knew the nigga would resist but to actually spit in your face... I'm sorry, David," Tesha said genuinely.

"Don't sweat it. He's dead. On to the next one," I said with single-minded determination.

Chapter 14
Four Days Later

"David, is that you?"

"Yeah, Ty, but go back to sleep, baby. Everything is alright," I replied, tiptoeing across the bedroom, making a beeline for the shower.

I quickly pulled off my clothes and was under the water's blistering hot spray within seconds, finally breathing a sigh of relief after escaping Tesha's clutches. It seemed like the more dirt we did in the streets, the more sexually insatiable she became, and that shit was becoming more than dangerous with all of us under the same roof. I'd adamantly refused to put my dick anywhere near her while we were inside the apartment with Ty and Tonya, so the compromise had been sneaking off for quickies. I'd played it smart and safe by not taking her to my other apartment in this building, or even letting anyone else know about that apartment, mainly because that apartment felt like all that I had left in this world that was mine. I damn sure wasn't about to fill that space with memories of women that I didn't see a forever with. Thankfully, this apartment building came equipped with a gym, a spa, a small movie theatre, and even a couple of restaurants, all of which gave me and Tesha places to link up. Before the sweat dried though, I was gone and back within the safe reaching distance of my future wifey.

Thankfully, Tonya hadn't made another move or play to get me back inside of her since our initial encounter, which meant that I only had to deal with one woman catching feelings. Tonya was giving me the knowing smirks whenever we were in the living room together, but I ignored the memories that surfaced of me pushing her face down into the couch and savagely fucking her. There had been no emotion in it for me, and I never intended for there to be. As much as I tried to make my time with Tesha about sexual fulfillment, I could tell that she was catching the vapors for me, and her nose was opening wider. I played it cool when we were all together, and when we were alone, I treated her like a smut so that she wouldn't fill her pretty little head with fantasies of a nigga who didn't exist. For the most part, I kept everyone's mind focused on the new business we'd built because our legacy was growing damn near overnight. The ways I'd left Taliban and Meiko had put the word savage in the same descriptive sentence of the person or people who pulled off the robbery/extermination at his house.

What I'd done to the next nigga we'd run down on would've been called biblical if the devil had written the Bible. The nigga, Lacy, had been from a small city in Northern Virginia, and he'd come to Florida on a chase for the money that Florida was known to have plenty of. Chasing the dream had made him feel entitled to what he'd "earned" down here, so I'd had to spend a little time torturing him until reality set in, and he remembered that the game giveth and the game taketh away. In the end, poor Lacy had ended up with bright red lipstick on his lips, his sparse dreadlocks spread out across the bed pillow I'd positioned him on, and his dick and balls sewed shut in between his snitching ass lips. Neither Ty nor Tesha had had the stomach to watch me work on him like that, but I'd been glad about that because I knew it would've changed their opinions of me.

As it stood now, they just looked at me with concern whenever the topic of pulling a lick came up. One thing that I could say for sure was that word had spread rapidly, and we'd robbed everyone else without issue. The streets were talking, and Zoe Pound definitely wanted blood, but it was Roland who owed the debt. Roland was running in circles, trying to figure out who had blown into town with the intent of taking over, but once he found out that Tynesha and Tesha were the culprits, he'd damn near had a mental breakdown.

Their phones rang nonstop until they got rid of them for new ones, but then, the calls started coming to my phone too. I wasted no time getting a new one after I'd had a civilized conversation with Roland. This wasn't some movie where I revealed our grand scheme only for it to be foiled in the end, so our conversation was mainly me taunting him until he screamed unintelligibly. The enjoyment I got from hearing that grown man lose his shit let me know that I was a cruel person, but I was okay with that. He should've played with Jesus instead of playing with me. When it was all said and done, we'd walked away with close to two million dollarss' worth of heroin, fentanyl, and cash, not to mention that twenty of their best female sex workers had been set free to vanish without a trace. Zoe Pound was hemorrhaging money, and the tensions that were created in the streets could be felt from Tallahassee to Fort Lauderdale and every city in between. This was just the beginning of the chess match, but I was trying to mentally fortify for the long haul. Dealing with life and death in these streets was easier than the emotional rollercoaster of Tesha, Tynesha, and Tonya, which was why I tried to always focus on business. Even underneath the water's spray, I could hear Ty moving around in the bedroom that we shared, which let me know that she was waiting to talk. This was the second night in a row I'd come home in the middle of the night, and I wasn't covered in blood, so that limited my explanations. I spent another ten minutes methodically washing my body, trying to figure out a plausible reason I'd been out late. Nothing as significant as curing cancer popped up in my mind as a defense, so I got out of the shower, mentally prepared to face the music. When

I came out of the bathroom, Ty was sitting up with her back against the headboard and a plate of food resting in between her thick thighs.

"I know you probably didn't eat, so I warmed up some leftover meatloaf and mashed potatoes."

"Thank you, baby. I'm actually starving," I confessed, sitting on the bed beside her.

I could tell that she would've been content to feed me, but I took the plate so that my hands stayed busy.

"You couldn't sleep again?"

"Nah, but I got a good workout in at the gym, and my body feels physically tired now," I replied.

"You could've woke me up, and I would've worked your body out righteously."

I chuckled appropriately as I began eating my food, but I could feel the tension building, and I wanted to counteract it.

"The night is still young, sweetheart," I said, giving her a knowing look.

"You know that good loving is that one free pass that you get for waking me up, keeping me up, or fucking my hair up so don't threaten me with a good time."

"I know that's right. Not many women have been able to keep up with me or match my freak level, but you've evenly matched so far. Don't get cocky because we're just getting started though, and I've been taking it slow with you." I informed her.

"Oh, really? Taking it slow? Baby, I'm ready, willing, and able to handle whatever you wanna throw my way just as long as it don't involve other people because I don't share."

The way she made the last statement struck me like a punch to the nose, and I was fighting against the water trying to invade my eyes. My guilt was sucking the oxygen out of my lungs and the room, which was why I had to change course quickly.

"Just remember that we have that in common and right now, Roland thinking that him and I can share you is why his ass is on fire. I act funny bout what's mine," I warned.

Her smile was both tempting and inviting, but thankfully, I was saved by the loud vibrations of my phone.

"Damn, bae, who blowing your shit up at this time of night?" she asked, picking my phone up off the nightstand.

"I don't know... answer it."

I knew that me telling her to pick up the phone would fuck her up in a good way, and the expression of shock on her face let me know that I'd caught her off guard.

"Answer it?" she repeated skeptically, holding the phone up in between us.

"I'm eating, bae, just answer it."

There were doubt and uncertainty crisscrossing her beautiful face, but it gave way to love as she smiled and pressed the talk button.

"Hello?" Ty said tentatively.

"Can I speak to King David?" a female with an accent asked politely.

Ty's eyebrow immediately shot up, and I knew that her first thought had to do with this woman on the other end of the phone addressing me as king. I didn't say shit or panic. I kept right on fucking up the delicious meatloaf while navigating the gravy with a Hawaiian dinner roll.

"King David is busy at the moment, but this is his woman, and I can take a message for him," Ty offered.

"Please tell him that his aunt and uncle have arrived in the United States, and he is expected to meet with them by 1 p.m. tomorrow at the Four Seasons hotel in Beverly Hills."

My fork froze in midair as I processed this new information rapidly, and then, I checked to see what time it was. Three in the morning here made it midnight on the west coast, which meant that my uncle was working late. I nodded my head in agreement.

"I'll makes sure he gets the message," Ty said.

"I suggest that you make sure he gets here," the woman replied, hanging up abruptly.

Suddenly, my appetite vanished, forcing me to put the fork down and push the still full plate away.

"David, what was all that about? What aunt and uncle was that lady on the phone referring to, and why did she refer to you as King David?"

I heard all of her questions, but none of them made it onto the highway of my brain because there were too many other thoughts fast moving in those lanes. My family coming to the United States without warning or known business didn't sit well with me, and the way my first cousin, Zipporah, spoke on the phone meant that me seeing them wasn't optional. A combination of these facts told me that my aunt and uncle were specifically here to see me, and their timing was anything but coincidental.

These were the oldest living relatives on my father's side of my DNA chain, and I hadn't met them until I was eighteen years old. With that monumental birthday came an unexpected inheritance, along with a tutorial about my family history stretching from the Ghana region of Africa all the way to the enslaved shores of North America. All my life, my mother had thought that she had been tricked by a nothing ass nigga who'd left her to raise me on her own, but in reality, he'd been ordered to come back home and defend his birth rights. We were descendants of royalty in Africa, and that still meant something there despite how the United States government had tried to eradicate our history for money.

Once I'd discovered the truth about my father, I made the trip home to a place I'd never been and visited my father's grave. He'd been a soldier, and he'd died fighting oppression in the Sudan, which meant he'd lived and died with honor. The bond that I'd forged with my family had been a strained one because my heart still held anger for my grandparents who made my father abandon my mother and me. Over time,

I'd realized that my anger helped no one, including myself, and if I held onto it, then I'd lose the last part of myself that I still needed to discover. So, I'd swallowed my pride and became a sponge for my heritage. In the years since I'd learned about my father's side of the family, I'd met and traced my bloodline deep into the Democratic Republic of the Congo. Times were different, but my lineage remained the same. If the day dawned when I so chose to renounce my American citizenship, I'd be welcomed home to the motherland with open arms and an official title. Despite my aunt and uncles not so subtle pushing, I had yet to renounce my rights as an African American, and I wasn't ready to leave for good.

I didn't know why exactly they were here, but no matter what their purpose was, they always somehow got around to mentioning me moving to Africa.

"David, are you listening?"

"Huh?" I replied, confused and caught off guard.

"WHAT is going on?"

"I don't know. I guess my aunt and uncle wanna see me," I replied, shrugging my shoulders.

"Yeah, I gathered that from the call you had me answer. Would you care to fill in the damn gaps to the story because there's obviously a lot missing," she said, clearly frustrated.

"It's a long story, bae, and right now, I need to find a red eye flight to get me to the west coast on time. I'll explain when I come back. I promise."

"Nah, man, fuck that! You got a call from a woman I don't know, telling you that you've been summoned across the goddamn country by some relatives I've never heard of, and you're just gonna hop your ass on a plane with a promise to explain later? Boy, you got me confused, twisted, bent, and fucked up," she said, hopping out of the bed and heading into our bedroom closet.

She kept mumbling to herself while she was in the closet, but all I could make out was the occasional cuss word followed by a manic sounding laugh that made my skin hot. I didn't have time to argue or fight with her, which would normally lead to me using sex as a distraction, but I didn't even have time for that. I knew that I had to give her something though, so I decided to multitask by arranging my travel plans using my phone and giving Ty an oral history lesson about my family.

"Babe, I'm sorry that this is all being sprung on you at the last minute, but I'll give you the short version. My pops was originally from Ghana, Africa, and my aunt and uncle are my family on his side. A few years ago..."

"You can tell me the rest later because I can't focus my thoughts on what you're saying. Just help me pack," she said, tossing some clothes at me followed by a duffel bag.

"Baby, your clothes are mixed in with mine."

"I know that, dummy. Just pack it all in the duffel and I'll put the important shit in my carry-on bag," she replied nonchalantly.

"Tynesha, you can't go with me..."

"I can, and I am going with you, or you ain't going. You choose," she said, peeking her head out of the closet to stare directly at me.

The fire in her eyes was lit from the coals of determination that I saw smoldering right next to the anger that was feeding it like oxygen. I was too smart to pick this fight with this woman, so I kept my lips shut and folded our clothes like I'd been instructed to do.

"Wise choice, King David. Wise fucking choice."

Chapter 15

We landed at LAX with a couple hours to spare and drove straight to the hotel so that we could freshen up to look presentable. I'd given Tynesha a run down on my father's brother, my Uncle Umar, and his first wife, my Aunt Zynefa, so that they at least wouldn't appear like complete strangers to her. They had been close to my father, which had allowed me to gain significant insight into the man he was growing up and who'd he been as a man when he'd come home from America. Their insight and knowledge helped me let the anger go when it came to him. He didn't just come home to be a toy soldier in the ongoing African civil war. He'd wanted someone to look after his elderly parents too. In the end, no one had been willing to treat his parents with the love, respect, and decency that he knew they deserved, so he'd taken that responsibility as a son should. In a way, I was just like him, and it was more so obvious in this situation with Ty because I was willing to do anything for her and with her. Our love story was happening now, and it felt like it was turning into something epic. At first, I'd thought that she'd insisted on coming with me just to keep tabs on me, but I immediately noticed the little things she was doing for me to make my life easier, whether it was renting a car and reserving our hotel room or making sure the stewardess kept the warm towels coming on the plane to keep me comfortable because I didn't like flying for real. Before my very eyes, I was watching a down ass bitch in the making, and it was a sight to behold.

"Bae, you can take your shower first while I order us some food. Is there anything you want in particular?" she asked.

"You can order whatever... And then join me in the shower," I replied, pulling my shirt off and heading in that direction.

I didn't hear her response, but the look of passion burning in her eyes was bright enough to light an entire major city. Something about being away from the stresses and drama we were under in Florida, combined with being alone without her sister and mom, had heightened my desire for her. I'd thought about making her a member of the mile high club on the flight here, but there was way too many people minding everything except their own business. I had her all to myself now though, and that put a smile on my face as I got completely naked. The shower head hung from above, like one you might see in an outdoor shower at the beach, and the water's pressure was perfect along with the temperature. I felt the stress rinse from my scalp and go straight down the drain at my feet with the water's flow, bringing me peace and relaxation within seconds. When I felt a soapy washcloth being gently applied to my back in small, slow circles, I let out a sigh of contentment mixed with hunger. I turned and pulled Ty into my arms, kissing her like it was my first time, and I wanted to make the right impression in her soul. I was tempted to back her into a wall and slide her up it to begin, but instead, I flexed my physical strength by picking her straight up and letting the water cascade over us while easing my dick up inside her. The trembling in her legs was immediate, but she still managed to wrap herself around me while I cradled her soft ass cheeks in my palms. Our rhythm was slow and exploratory, becoming deeper with each stroke as her pussy molded to me like the hands of a sculptor manipulating his moist clay.

Moans of passion were released around kisses from the shared hunger between our tongues. I could feel our heartbeats calling to each other, challenging us to a race as the temperature continued rising, turning the water on our bodies into lustful steam. Her arms followed her legs, increasing our closeness while giving her leverage to climb the tree that my hard wood represented. Her heat was radiating from inside out, and with each stroke, I pushed us closer to the sun because her pussy was the portal to life's force. I willingly lost myself in her and to her, surrendering to what we needed as I spun her into the nearest wall so that I could fuck her faster and harder. I could feel the flesh of my back yield to her fingernails, giving up blood as she dug in deliberately, and it brought more pleasure than pain. When I felt her teeth sink into my neck, I bucked like a bull underneath the branding iron, and in that move, I knocked the head off of her sprinkler which caused her to drench my dick with her cum. The way her pussy's grip intensified with the brief intermissions in squeezing like a strobe light triggered my own climax, and I came hard. The wall barely held us both up, but somehow, I managed not to fall.

"Th-That was different," she panted, unwrapping her legs from around me so that she could attempt standing up.

"R-Right. A-Amazing though."

Her chuckle turned into infectious laughter that left us both giddy and clearly satisfied. I picked up the washcloth that she had dropped, and then, I bathed her sensually before passing it to her so that she could return the favor. Once we finally emerged from our man-made cocoon, we found the food waiting for us in the room, and I made her relax on the bed while I brought it to her. We fed each other lobster tails dipped in delicious garlic butter sauce and chatted about nothing the way that new couples do when they're just enamored with their partner's presence. After we finished our impromptu lunch date, we got dressed, and then, I mentally made the adjustment for the sit down that was about to happen. I probably could've left Ty in the room, but I knew that would've hurt her feelings and our relationship, and I didn't want that. To my way of thinking, this was my way to kill two birds with one stone because she was meeting my family, and that was always an important step. While I waited on Ty to finish up the girly things she was doing in the bathroom, I sent a text to my uncle, letting him know that we were here and asking where he wanted to meet. He immediately responded by giving me his room number.

"My aunt and uncle are in the penthouse of this hotel. Are you ready?"

"As I'll ever be," she replied, coming out of the bathroom looking runway model fresh with a freshly fucked glow.

I stood there for a moment, not even trying to hide the heat from my stare, as I drank her in from her manicured toes in the white, open toed, wedge sandals and up her white and red sundress that held her curves like a safety harness. With her hair piled high on top of her head in a messy bun, her graceful neck stood out, giving her a refined elegance that I'd noticed before in professional dancers. The way she was put together made her seem effortlessly regal to me, and I knew what impression she would leave on my aunt and uncle.

"Wow, bae...wow," I said, smiling like my teeth had a mind of their own.

"Thank you. This dress doesn't show too much of my titties, does it?"

"Nah, you're good," I replied quickly, licking my lips unconsciously.

Her laughter was genuine, and it made me feel warm inside. I made sure we had everything we needed, and then, I led the way to the elevators. Five minutes later, I was standing before my uncle, Umar, being pulled into a bear hug that was strong enough to crack a few ribs. I didn't have time to warn Ty about what was about to happen to her before my uncle had passed me on to my aunt, Zynefa, and his burly body was threatening to swallow her completely.

"It's good to see you again, David. Your uncle and I have missed you."

"I missed you too, Auntie, and I was still planning to meet you two in Ghana for the holidays. You didn't have to come all this way."

"Didn't we?" my uncle asked from behind me.

When I turned to face him, I saw the seriousness in his expression, and I knew that I was in some kind of trouble.

"Come, we have much to discuss," Umar said, leading the way into the lavish living room.

Ty and I sat on the plush loveseat adjacent to the matching couch, and somehow, our hands instantly ended up together with our fingers linked. Her palm was soft and not sweaty, which helped me to regulate my body's temperature. I wanted to go on offense and explain myself before Uncle dug in my ass, but I knew that letting him speak was the quickest way to get this over with.

"David, when you and I last spoke, what did we discuss?" Umar asked, taking a seat on the couch beside my aunt.

"We talked about my future and the fact that I need to take it more serious if I wanted my life to be about anything."

"Precisely, and do you feel like you've adequately applied the wisdom that your aunt and I dispensed on you during that conversation?" he asked.

I looked from my uncle to my aunt and then to my left where Tynesha sat quietly, holding my hand.

"I absolutely take my life and future more seriously now," I replied, smiling at Ty while gently squeezing her hand.

"Killing is a serious business, but your willingness to do that doesn't mean that you aren't living in a fantasy world," he stated.

I felt the smile vanish from my lips as the sobering effect of his words took root in my mind.

"David, your uncle and I have never judged you for the ways in which you have chosen to live your life, no matter how much we felt that you were wasting your time and talents. This has been your life to live, and we have merely watched from the sidelines, but now, you have forced us into action."

"How so, Auntie?" I asked, confused.

"Because you have made enemies of very powerful people. This detective, Roland Simms, is but a pawn on the chess board, but his allies move with the unseen hands of power. Power that you have threatened by weakening and exposing their operational flaws with your flagrant disregard for human life," Umar replied.

"We know that this started as a noble gesture of you trying to protect the woman you have come to love, but now... now you seem hell bent on destroying this man, Roland Simms, and yourself in the process," Zynefa said.

"When you declare war, it's kill or be killed. Period," I replied unapologetically.

"You think to lecture us on the principles of war, young man?" Umar asked in a lethal whisper.

"David would never be so bold or disrespectful as to lecture either of you. From what he told me, he respects you and his family a great deal, and because of that, you should know that nothing he's done has been for shits and giggles. Roland will not leave me alone, and now, he's just as obsessed with David, which left us no choice except to go after him harder than he would expect," Ty explained calmly.

"But are you willing to endure the same consequences for David as he is for you?" Umar asked her pointedly.

"Without hesitation. I love him," Ty declared, holding my hand tighter.

My tongue got stuck to the roof of my mouth, and my heart was beating hard enough for me to feel it in my shoelaces. Her words moved me. I knew how I felt inside, and in my heart, I'd wanted to believe that she had felt the same way about me, but to hear her actually verbalize it made my heart sing with joy. I had to work extra hard to contain it though and stay focused on the here and now.

"You speak of love easy enough, but real love requires dedication, trust, and above all else, it requires sacrifice. What are you willing to sacrifice, young lady?" Zynefa asked.

"I will sacrifice my world and everything in it for David," Ty replied.

"Be careful with your words, Tynesha, because you will be required to stand on them when you're talking to us," Umar warned.

Ty looked at me in a way that melted my soul as she brought my hand to her lips and kissed it gently.

"I wouldn't say it if I didn't mean it," Ty stated genuinely.

"Excuse us for a moment," Zynefa said, taking my uncle by the hand and pulling him to his feet.

They quietly left the room, and as soon as they were out of sight, I pulled her into my arms so that I could display my passion with action. I kissed her fast and thoroughly, and by the time I pulled back, she was halfway in my lap, panting with sexual frustration.

"Damn, boy, I would've told you that I love you sooner had I known this was gonna be your response. Most niggas run from love," she said, laughing.

"Yeah, well, I love you too, and I just wanted that to be clear."

"I'm starting to get the picture, but you're more than welcome to show me more when we get back to the room," she offered seductively.

"Indeed, I will. Listen though, I don't want you to feel any pressure from my aunt and uncle. They mean well, but there's a lot that I feel like they don't understand about this situation."

"Then I'm in the same boat because I definitely feel like there's something I'm missing about your family. How would they be so well informed about what we're doing in Florida when they're all the way in Africa?" she asked logically.

"The short answer is because they're heavily invested in the import/export business in the U.S., and Florida is a major hub of activity. They deal in everything from cars to jewels and gold... along with other more questionably legal things like weapons, explosives, and black-market medical drugs. You gotta remember that the United States never had the market cornered on government corruption. They just choose to lie about their bullshit. Africa is more of something that's understood when it comes to getting things and getting things done by any means necessary."

Her response was to chuckle and nod her head in understanding, but I saw no judgement in her eyes. That made me feel relief about telling the truth. I'd have to ask her how she truly felt later because my aunt and uncle walked back into the living room, clearly on some serious shit.

"Stand up, David," Umar demanded.

I did as I was instructed, feeling a bit apprehensive at the tone of voice he was using.

"Yes, Uncle?"

"As my nephew, I can protect you to the fullest extent of my powers, and my reach is quite long within the circles you choose to associate yourself with. My protection capabilities stop with you though," he stated, looking pointedly at Ty before turning his penetrating gaze back on me.

"I understand, Uncle, and I will protect those that I love."

He stared at me long and hard for a moment before taking my hand and placing something in my palm. Out of the corner of my eye, I saw Zynefa doing the same thing with Ty.

"And so you shall," Umar said ominously.

We opened our hands at the same time, and what I saw made me look straight over at Ty. I found her eyes locked with mine, and in them formed a silent understanding that was hard for either of us to grasp.

"Uncle Umar... What is this?" I asked slowly, searching his face intensely.

"That in your hand is the first ring that your aunt, Zynefa, gifted me to symbolize our marriage."

"And that is the very first wedding band that Umar gave to me when we were married years ago," Zynefa said, her voice crackling with sentiment.

"Okay... so, you want us to have them?" Ty asked.

"Only if you plan to use them," Umar replied.

"Meaning what?" I asked.

"My husband is an ordained minister, Tynesha. So, do you take King David Bishop to be your lawfully wedded husband from this day forward?"

Chapter 16
One Week Later - Florida

"You mind telling me how the fuck you two found the time to take a goddamn vacation in the middle of the war that you two started?!" Tonya yelled as soon as we stepped foot inside my apartment.

"We missed you too, Mom," Tynesha replied sarcastically.

"Little bitch, don't get smart because you ain't never too grown for an ass whooping," Tonya threatened.

"Chill out, Tonya, damn," I said, dropping our bags by the door and locking everything up tight behind us.

"Nigga, was I talking to you?" Tonya asked, taking a step toward me.

"Mom," Ty said in warning, taking a step in between us.

"What the fuck is going on out here?" Tesha asked, coming into the room wearing nothing but an oversized, blue T-shirt.

"Look who finally decided to come back after they left us for dead for a whole fucking week," Tonya said, still staring at me with a mixture of anger and contempt.

"Mom, don't you think that you're being a little dramatic? You act like we left you in the middle of a warzone somewhere in Iraq," Ty said.

"You might as well have! Your nigga was running all around Orlando dropping bodies like the new plague, and then, you two got ghost before the retaliation can come.

That's some real fuck shit," Tonya said, clearly disgusted with us.

"Not that I owe you an explanation, considering the fact that I saved your life and I'm letting you relax comfortably in my own private fortress, but Tynesha and I went out of town for business. It was important business, and it was necessary to what we've got going on down here."

"Why didn't you tell us? You didn't call, and you barely texted, so we don't know what was really going on," Tesha said.

"And I'm sorry about that, but we were busy. Plus, David assured me that you had everything you could need here, so we figured you grown ass women could survive a few days without us," Ty stated, fighting to remain calm in the face of this inquisition.

"Obviously nobody got in here, so what's wrong? Did you run out of chocolate?" I asked, chuckling.

"Fuck you, David," Tesha replied, following her words with the traditional hand gesture.

"I missed you too, Tesha," I said, winking at her.

The way she blushed and avoided looking directly at me meant that I was forgiven by one half of the dynamic duo, but the look on Tonya's face wasn't promising forgiveness. She was too busy staring at Ty to give a fuck about me, so I took that as my cue to grab our bags and unpack.

"I'ma put this stuff away, baby, and then, I'll fix us a late lunch," I said, heading toward our bedroom.

I didn't wait for Ty's response, but as soon as I was out of sight, I heard all three of their voices in a heated exchange. It was times like this that let me know that I had to be the craziest nigga alive to actually be living under the same roof with all of them simultaneously. I tossed the contents of our duffel bags in the bed, and then, I quickly separated the clean from the dirty clothes. We'd had to buy a few things when we were out in L.A., due to the unexpected extra time spent in that California sunshine, but I didn't mind spending a few dollars on my lady. The wedding present of $100K that my aunt and uncle had given us was still safely in the bank, untouched, because I'd wanted to shower my wife with gifts from the fruits of my own labors. Despite our newfound closeness, I still hadn't found a way to tell her that we were financially straight for the rest of our lives. There were a lot of secrets that I was looking forward to sharing with her, if for no other reason than to have someone to finally bare my soul to. I stopped messing with the clothes long enough to gaze down at the ring on my left ring finger, and right away, I got the same giddy feeling that I had every day since we had exchanged vows. At first, I'd thought that my uncle and my aunt had lost their damn minds for even recommending a move so bold, but once it started to make sense, I couldn't shake the happiness I felt expanding through my body. In truth, we had spent time during our trip to focus on business, but we'd mainly been enjoying married life. I'd never thought I'd be so easily domesticated, but I actually loved being Tynesha's husband. The only problem that either of us had seen so far was how we would explain our moves to other people, mainly her mom and sister. I was nervous for different reasons than she was though because I knew that my individual indiscretions with both of those women would put them in a different emotional state with this truth.

I had no idea how I was going to put the words together, but that honestly wasn't even my most pressing issue. Now that I was back in town, and I had the okay from my uncle, it was time to attack Roland head on. The only catch was leaving Zoe Pound businesses alone. I didn't know what that would look like, but it would happen sooner rather than later. I finished separating clothes and unpacking before making my way to the kitchen to make us something to eat. The sounds of three hens still clucking could be heard, but I knew to leave that alone and mind my business. Going to the refrigerator, I thankfully found everything I needed to whip up a couple mushroom omelets, and I got to work on them while my mind reviewed possible battle plans. Like my uncle had said, Roland was a pawn in this game, but I knew that this had the potential to make him the most dangerous piece on the board. A pawn could shape shift into anything the game's master needed it to be once he had it positioned in just the right spot. I knew now that if ever I'd run into a nigga who defined that, it was Roland Simms. The only advice that Umar and Zynefa had given us before we left was to get this war over with as quickly as possible because the longer a wounded Roland was allowed to roam, the more dangerous and deadly he became. As I finished up mine and Tynesha's omelets, I made a mental checklist of the phone calls I needed to make sooner rather than later.

"Oh, my God, they're gonna drive me fucking loco, and we've only been here a few minutes," Ty exclaimed, coming into the kitchen and sitting on the counter.

I put her plate of food in front of her and kissed her gently on the top of her head.

"You say the word and we'll stay somewhere else," I whispered.

"Thanks, bae, but you said it yourself. There's nowhere safer that we could be right now than this building. So, unless you've got another apartment in this building, we're stuck with your annoying ass In-laws."

Before I could stop it, laughter leaped from my throat, and it was uncontrollable for real.

"What's so damn funny?" she asked with a confused expression on her face.

I shook my head as if it was nothing while I put my own omelet on a plate and sat next to her. I could feel her staring at me as I began eating, but I still avoided eye contact.

"Son of a bitch," she whispered, poking me hard in the chest with her trigger finger.

"Ow! What was that for?"

"Because your slick ass has another fucking apartment in this building, and you didn't think to have us there instead of in hell with two of the devil's keepers," she continued in a furious whisper.

All I could do was laugh, but the look that she gave me told me to shut that shit up, so I suppressed it by putting food in my mouth.

"Un-fucking-believable, David! I know one thing; you better have us moved in there by the end of the day, or the kitchen is closed to this good pussy that you love so much. You're on a diet, my nigga, with no cheat days," she said seriously.

I choked on a piece of egg that went down the wrong tube, and for some reason, that made her giggle. She didn't even have the decency to pat me on the back. She just started eating while humming.

"Mmm, babe, this is good, but it's missing a little something," she said as she got up and went to the refrigerator.

I wanted to cuss her ass out so bad that I was tempted to spit my food out just to do it, but I resisted that temptation. When she sat back down and began to drip chocolate syrup all over her omelet, the laughter died in my throat, and suddenly, the coughing fit was over.

"Uh, bae, do you realize that you grabbed Hershey's chocolate syrup?" I asked slowly.

"Of course I realize it, dumb dumb, and it tastes good as fuck."

She emphasized her point by taking a huge bite, but Tesha picked that moment to enter the kitchen.

"What smells so good? And where is mine at?" Tesha asked.

The speed with which Ty transferred my omelet to her plate and shot her elbows out so that she was eating with all the protectiveness of a convict made me laugh hard.

"Damn, bitch, I can't even get a piece?" Tesha asked, clearly offended.

"Nope, sorry," Ty replied unapologetically.

"David, will you make me one?" Tesha asked sweetly, moving in my direction.

I was about to agree, just to keep the peace, but the look Ty shot in my direction said it all.

"Nope, sorry. I've gotta clean up and go to a meeting wit a guy about a thing," I replied, gathering the trash off the counters and tossing it in the can under the sink.

The trash bag filled up quickly, so I pulled it out and took it out into the hallway where the trash shoot in the wall led downstairs to the incinerator. When I went to lift the bag, something caught my eye that made me drop the bag altogether and take a flinching step backwards. Paranoia caused me to look up and down the hallway as if eyes were on me, lock onto my movements, and add them up to spell out my guilt. I didn't see anyone, of course, but I could still see a corner of the box that had startled me through the trash bag. After taking a few deep breaths to steady my galloping heart, I reached inside the bag, pulled the box out, and dropped the bag at my feet. The words on the box were in plain English, but suddenly, I couldn't read at the level of a first grader, let alone a high school graduate. I couldn't count how many times I'd seen the pink and white FIRST RESPONSE pregnancy test in supermarkets and corner stores, but never had I held one, and I damn sure never had a reason to have one in my apartment. My brain checked every hiding spot and secret passageway that my mind was comprised of, but I found no logical explanation to hang my hat on except for the one I didn't like. It was obvious that the box had been opened, which meant that the pregnancy test had been taken, but the box didn't feel empty. Against my better judgement, I peeked inside, and sure enough, the used pee stick was in there as if someone thought that this would hide the truth. I pulled it out, looked at it, put it back, and then read the instructions on the side of the box. Twice. It felt like I was in a trance as I walked back into my apartment and shut the door, but all I knew was that I had to keep moving to avoid falling apart. When I came into the kitchen, I found Tynesha still eating, and Tesha was at the stove with Tonya whipping something up. I sat the box on the counter next to Ty, which caused her to immediately drop her fork and look up like a frightened deer that somehow ended up in the interstate.

"Wh-Where did that come from, David?" Ty asked.

I turned to face Tesha and Tonya, but neither of them were paying attention.

"Mom?" Ty called out.

When Tonya looked up, her eyes immediately locked in on the pink box.

And then, she nudged Tesha.

"Ty... I was gonna tell you, but I didn't wanna do it through text," Tesha explained.

"Y-You're pregnant?" I asked hollowly.

"Yeah, she is," Tonya replied, looking right at me with some smug type of satisfaction.

"Oh, no," Ty said softly, shaking her head as if she was trying to deny the truth.

"It's okay, Ty. I'll be fine. My baby will be fine," Tesha assured her even though her eyes were locked on me.

"It's not that... it's just… our periods. We've been in sync for months," Ty said, sounding utterly lost.

"Tynesha..." Tonya said, looking suddenly concerned.

"I'm late, Mom... I didn't get my period at all in the last week... which means..."

"You're pregnant too," I said softly.

Chapter 17

The way Tynesha bolted off of the bar stool at the counter had me looking around for an active shooter situation because baby was gone gone. Tonya followed behind her, no doubt to offer support and calm her fucked up nerves, but that left me and Tesha alone in the kitchen, staring at each other a few feet away like there was an ocean between us.

"No disrespect but..."

"It's yours, David, so don't ask no dumb shit that'll get you smacked right now," she said in a low tone.

"I thought you were on birth control or that you were gonna take a Plan B."

"I forgot to regularly take my birth control because I wasn't fucking nobody until you came along, and the Plan B obviously didn't work," she replied, moving closer to me so that she could maintain her low tone of voice.

"Okay, so what's the plan now?"

"Explain what you mean, David, but choose your fucking words carefully, my nigga."

"This ain't the time for no muthafuckin hand holding and choosing words carefully. Are you having the baby or not?" I asked blatantly.

"Why the fuck wouldn't I?"

"Do I really need to list the reasons?" I asked sarcastically.

"Not unless you plan on giving my sister the same pep talk when she comes back in this bitch cause you ain't never gonna play me like her baby is better than mine."

The anger inside of her was causing her voice to go up an octave and tremble, and I needed it not to do that, so I did choose my next words carefully.

"That's not what I'm saying or what I'm implying. I was simply trying to find out if you're mentally prepared to be a single mother," I said calmly.

"And my response is still are you gonna ask Tynesha that same question? If not, then don't bring that shit to me either because you WILL help me raise this baby. I put that on God, my nigga."

Tonya came back into the kitchen with a preoccupied look on her face, but it was clear to see that she recognized the tension that she walked into. I didn't know if Tesha knew that her mom had recorded us having sex that night because she'd heard me creep in. I just knew that Tonya knew I had put a baby in both of her daughters, and that was dangerous information to be in possession of. It could hurt me, but that same shit could get Tonya killed. I kept that to myself though as she came right over to me and put her lips to my ear.

"You better be one hell of a nigga because you're stuck with us for life... or until death. You choose," she whispered before gently kissing my ear lobe.

I desperately wanted to backhand her ass right in the mouth, but she made a business decision and got out of the way by going back to her position beside Tesha. I left them both there, talking amongst themselves, and I went in search of my wife to give her all the support she deserved. For the moment, I had to swallow my guilt because it had no place here, and it would be selfish of me to lose myself when others needed me. I found Ty sitting on our bed, slowly rocking back-and-forth with her arms wrapped around her midsection like she was physically protecting her and the unborn baby. Our unborn baby.

"Ty... sweetheart, are you okay?"

She looked up at me with tears of confusion in her eyes, and it broke my heart to see anything other than her joy in this moment.

"Are-Are you alright, David? I mean, you went from single and living the bachelor life to married with a kid on the way faster than a nigga could pull the trigger. I love you, David, I really do, but trapping you wasn't..."

"Girl, hush up with that talk because you didn't trap me. Baby, you've blessed me more than I have a right to ask for, and I'm so grateful for that," I said, sitting beside her and pulling her into my arms.

I felt her sigh of relief, and it gave me some sense of peace because I now knew what to do in order to make things better for her. Right now, that meant just holding her and rocking with her.

"I'm scared, bae," she confessed in a voice so soft that I almost missed it.

"I got you... and we can be scared together."

"You ain't scared of shit," she replied.

"Except for your moms."

This made us both laugh, and we cracked jokes about what type of grandmother she would be. I could feel the tension start to dissipate from Ty's body, and her heartbeat synced at a calming rate with my own, which told me that we would be good. It was more important than ever before to keep us that way.

"David, I know you didn't ask, but the baby is yours, not Roland's."

She leaned back to look up at me and gauge my response for herself.

"The thought or question never crossed my mind, bae. I swear."

"Well, still, I just wanted to be clear because I don't need that hanging over us. I'll gladly take a DNA test when..."

"Baby, just chill. I told you that none of that is necessary," I said, smiling at her.

"Okay. Now that we've got that settled, I need to go find out who the fuck got my sister pregnant because that nigga better step up to the plate."

Her words caused me a moment's panic, but I controlled it using logic and necessary distraction.

"No disrespect to your sister or her baby, but we got a more pressing issue to deal with. You know like I do that Roland ain't gonna believe that you ain't carrying his baby, and that is only gonna make him more unpredictable. We've gotta eliminate him as soon as possible," I said seriously.

"You're right. I wasn't even thinking about that. The news of my pregnancy can be used to our advantage though."

"How's that?" I asked cautiously.

"It'll lure him out and make him vulnerable. From there, we just have to get someone to take him out, but it can't be you, David. I can't have you go down for capital murder when I'm preparing to bring your son or daughter into the world, so we need to find someone else to drop the hammer on Roland."

"It would have to be someone we can trust and preferably someone he wouldn't suspect," I replied.

"The look on your face says that you've got the right someone in mind so spit it out."

I let the name in my mind turn over a few more times as I weighed the pros and cons of involving the female that I was thinking about. She was definitely crazy enough, and her loyalty would never be in question, but the history that I shared with her was complicated at the least.

"Who, David?"

"Shaomi," I replied, more than a little reluctantly.

"Shaomi... as in my cousin, Shaomi... your ex-girlfriend from high school? That Shaomi?"

"You know that's exactly who I'm talking about, which was why I didn't want to say it," I stated, shaking my head.

"Nah, you good, but I'ma need you to make it make sense."

"Beyond a doubt, we know that she's with the shit, and she's capable of rocking a nigga to sleep. Plus, she's your family, so her loyalty ain't in question," I replied.

"You don't think your opinion is biased because you were fucking her? I mean, yeah, she's cute, but who has she rocked to sleep?"

I knew that answering the question asked would expose more of my relationship than anyone besides me and Shaomi knew, but it was necessary to speak a little truth sometimes. A very little. Thinking about my ex sent my mind backwards in time, and I was remembering how shocked I'd been when Shaomi's 5'1", one hundred fifteen pounds, little ass had rocked off on a nigga in a school hallway who had grabbed her by the arm because she ignored him. The nigga she hit was a star running back for our school, standing 6'0",, and he weighed at least two hundred twenty pounds of solid muscle. When lil mama hit that little button on his chin though, he'd folded up like wrinkled jeans with no starch. From that point, she'd jumped on his muthafuckin head and wore his braids out, even leaving a couple of them on the floor. It was so sexy to me to see her get down without hesitation that I hadn't realized how truly beautiful she was until we went on our first date. We'd been damn near inseparable until she'd moved to Georgia in the middle of the school year, but she'd been back in Florida for like a year now. I just hadn't had a reason to reach out to her and being awkward wasn't really my thing.

"Listen, I've seen Sha Sha put work in, and I've put work in with her, so I know she's about that action. Not to mention the fact that she's always up for a new adventure, and this will be right up her alley when everything is explained," I said.

"What about when you explain us? Is she gonna respect that because, cousin or no cousin, I'll fuck a bitch up when it comes to you."

I knew that Ty's threat was real despite the smile it put on my face and the warm feeling it created in my chest.

"Baby, I'm not playing with my life, and our relationship will be respected at all costs. Trust me," I said softly, pulling her close to me so that I could press my lips to hers.

For a moment, our kiss made both of us forget everything we'd been talking about, and the heat between us was about to get hotter. At the last second though, I was able to pull back and stand up to create some distance.

"Where you going, husband?"

"I uh-I need to put these plans in motion," I stammered.

Her laughter let me know how disheveled I must've looked, but I wasn't even embarrassed. I was horny as fuck!

"It's all fun and games until I make you beg," I warned.

"You're right, and I'm sorry. Go ahead and handle the business and then come back to handle me... in our own apartment, right?"

"Unit 1218. Your fingerprints will let you in, and then, you can get it ready," I said, pulling her to her feet and kissing her forehead gently.

"You do know how to make a girl feel like a queen, and I love you for it. I'll show you just how much later on so be safe out there and come back to me in a hurry. I'll be waiting... naked."

"Whatever you say, my queen," I replied, smiling as I turned to leave.

I managed to make it out of the apartment without running into Tonya or Tesha, but I could still feel the weight of my sins on my chest. Even after I was sitting in my car with the engine running, my mind and my heart couldn't shake the ramifications of my decisions and how everybody's lives were affected. I knew I couldn't let myself go too far down the rabbit holes of guilt or self-pity because

I had to put all my energy into keeping everyone safe. When I finally pulled out of the parking garage, I headed to the restaurant I'd heard that Shaomi was working in as a hostess. A half hour later, I was walking through the front doors of Mama Son's Southern Soul Food restaurant, and I came face-to-face with a love familiar.

"Not David B, Mr. Break a Bitch's Heart, popping up on me at work," Shaomi said, putting her hand to the white, casual blouse she was wearing, feigning heart troubles.

"In the flesh. I figured that I'd come see you since you've been back in Florida for a while now and somehow managed to successfully avoid me."

"Avoid you? Boy, please. I ain't been thinking about you enough to need to avoid you, and you know it. So, how about we cut through the bullshit guilt trips and reverse psychology, and you tell me what you need from me because it's obvious that you want something?" she stated with an expectant look on her face.

Her beautiful, brown eyes still held that blazing fire which always made her appear bigger than her small size. My nickname for her had been C-4 because she packed that kind of punch, but I knew that reminiscing and using pet names would only piss her off. She was one of the most blunt, abrasive people that I'd met, and it suited her well.

It was never wise to try to play her or play with her, so my only option was to shoot straight. There were no customers in the restaurant, but there were workers setting up for the lunch rush. I motioned for her to follow me out into the alcove where patrons waiting to be seated stood, and I got down to business.

"Look, I might need your help to get a nigga so that I can stop him from breathing because he's a threat to me and your cousins."

"A few weeks back, I saw a Facebook Live post that Tynesha made... does this have something to do with that?"

she asked, using low tones and glancing around to make sure we were out of earshot.

"That's exactly what it's about. I need a face not familiar to him who's willing to pull the trigger without hesitation, even knowing the consequences."

She stared up at me in quiet contemplation, but her eyes didn't give me a hint as to which way she was leaning. Shaomi wasn't the type who killed for the fuck of it or for money as a primary motivator. She would erase a nigga for principle though, and she was fiercely protective of the things and people that she loved.

"Do you have a plan?" she asked.

"Nah, not really."

She chuckled ruefully at that while shaking her head.

"Same ole David, leap and then look. I'll take an early lunch and meet you in the parking lot in ten minutes. Oh, and David, don't even think to ask for some of this good pussy because I'm even more stingy than you remember. Under no circumstances can you and I get emotionally involved again. That almost killed me once... I won't make that same mistake."

Chapter 18

I sat in my car and waited patiently, trying to work on my sales pitch while I organized the other moving parts to this situation. All my eggs weren't in one basket, but the biggest part of the play was to eliminate Roland's supporting cast, so that was what I focused on while waiting on Shaomi. The videos that we'd spliced together were sent to the right people, who would get them to Zoe Pound, but the most convincing evidence was the note I'd sent with it. I offered my humblest apologies while insisting that I didn't know I was robbing Zoe Pound because Roland neglected to pass along that information. Proof of this was my willingness to give back every dollar stolen and make amends for the lives senselessly taken while defending what was rightfully Zoe Pound's. The nail in the coffin was my offer to bring Roland's head to Zoe Pound leadership, and all I was asking in return was a free pass for myself and my family. I made sure to bring my Uncle Umar up to speed on the moves I was making, but I also let him know that things had gotten more complicated because I had kids on the way. I was just finishing up that text when my passenger door opened, and Shaomi slid onto the seat beside me.

"Let's go for a ride," she suggested.

I started the car and pulled off with no destination in mind, but I was alert for possible threats or people following us. Neither one of us spoke for the first few minutes, and I was okay with that because I was just trying to get a feel for her without being awkward.

"I learned a lot from you, David, and that's part of the reason that I have no regrets when it comes to our relationship. We were a necessary experiment. One of the things that I learned from you was to question weird shit distrustfully, so I'm sure that you can guess where my mind is when you pull up out the blue, asking me to drop a nigga. A cop at that."

"Tynesha is pregnant," I blurted out.

For a moment, neither of us spoke, and then, I felt her studying my profile with an intense stare.

"She's pregnant... And you're desperate. That's probably the only thing you could've told me to make any sense of this shit. So, the baby is yours or the cops?"

My response was the look that I shot at her because some questions didn't matter while others didn't need to be asked.

"Why come to me? I mean, you've gotta see how that wasn't the best idea you ever had," she said, smirking.

"Because you're wise beyond your twenty years of age, so I knew you'd assess the situation clinically versus cynically... And because I'm desperate, like you pointed out."

"The truth looks good on you, David," she replied, laughing out loud.

"Fuck you very much."

"We've done that already, sweetheart. You couldn't handle the pussy then, and I know damn well you couldn't handle it now. More importantly though, if I do decide to help you with this little problem, then the last thing you should ever do is fuck me. I mean that," she warned.

When I locked eyes with her, I saw the girl that I used to know deep down, but now, the new woman that she had become was standing in front of that girl, protecting her. I could respect that, but I wasn't dumb enough to turn my back on that woman because a twinkle in her eyes was deadly in a familiar way.

"I hear you loud and clear," I replied.

"Okay, so let's discuss my price."

"Oh, so doing it for family ain't enough?" I asked, smiling.

"It might've been had my first love not stuck his dick in that family and created a baby. I grew up like sisters with Tynesha and Tesha, and the girl code says that you're off limits because you're my ex. And because they should've cared how I'd feel about it. It don't matter how many years ago you and I were together or even how our relationship ended. All that matters is the girl code, and it was violated, so this is business, and my price is $100K, nonnegotiable."

"I hear you... I just need a little time to get that much money together," I replied.

"Who are you lying to, David? You're forgetting that I'm one of the few people who knows the real you. I probably know you better than Tynesha's stuck-up ass ever will! That means I know you've got money stashed all over the place, not to mention your side hustle of robbing dope boys."

The last part of her statement got my attention enough for me to quickly pull over to the side of the road and throw the car in park.

"How the fuck do you know what I may or may not be out here in these streets doing?" I asked, projecting the hostility and suspicion I felt in the tone of my question.

"Calm the fuck down, big nigga. You act like the streets don't talk or something, and I know because I'm out here in these streets erryday! I know damn well that my scary ass cousins ain't turn into DMX overnight, so as soon as you told me that you got Ty pregnant, I did the math to the shit I been hearing. Are you gonna lie to my face and act like you ain't the nigga dropping bodies across Orlando? Or have you really forgotten that I used to ride with your crazy ass into hell without hesitation?"

"Have you ever known me to do some shit like what you're describing?" I countered.

"The robbery part, no, but sending a nigga to the afterlife to keep the fires lit... only if he or she deserved it. I don't know what the whole situation is or how my cousins are involved, but if you want me to step out here into this bullshit, then you can pay me what I want because I got responsibilities too. If not, you can drop me off at work and have a nice fucking day."

I wanted to smack her ass as hard as I could from front to back because her arrogance was as annoying as it was sexy. I didn't put my hands on her though. I just put the car back in drive and smoked the tires as we pulled off. For three blocks, we rode in silence with only the sounds of the Hemi under my hood speaking to the building anger in my chest. I was really trying to figure out what the fuck I was mad at though! Intellectually, I knew that the anger was irrational, and that was why I forced myself to let it go and focus on the important shit.

"I'll get you your money by later today. How do you want it?" I asked as politely as I could manage.

"Preferably in a legal bank account so that it can be inherited if I die behind this shit or end up in prison."

"I'll arrange it and meet you with the information later. What time do you get off from work?" I asked, preparing to make a U-turn and retrace our route.

"I'm already off. I quit before I came outside to meet you."

When I looked over at her quizzically, she just shrugged her shoulders and laughed.

"I knew you had to be desperate to come see me, plus I knew that you would only be about a play that was lucrative, so my life was gonna be forever changed by you again, and I accepted that," she explained, using uncanny insight and logic.

I couldn't be mad at how her mind worked, so I let it go.

"Do you need to go back and get your car from the restaurant?"

"No, my mom dropped me off because I'm kinda in between vehicles right now," she admitted.

"Are you staying with your ma?"

"Yeah, in the same old house where you and I used to... but you can drop me off at the gas station up the street so that I can grab a few things that we need at the house," she said.

I hung a left on New Haven Avenue and rode it out to Brightside Road, remembering the times I'd brought her home before and snuck into her bedroom. When I looked over at her, I caught the look of nostalgia creasing her features, and it made me laugh.

"Shut up and stay out of my head, David."

"I didn't say anything, Sha Sha."

"You don't have to say anything because the fact that you just called me Sha Sha says it all, nigga!" she replied, laughing with me.

It had been an honest slip of the tongue because I'd already convinced myself not to be too comfortable or familiar with her. For everyone's safety, I just kept my mouth closed and turned on the radio to allow for the distraction of music. By the time I pulled up to the Wawa gas station, we were both rapping along to MoneyBagg Yo like we'd grown up with him in the projects of Memphis. We exchanged phone numbers before she got out with the promise to link back up in a few hours. Instead of pulling off when she walked into the store, I'd waited, and when she came back out, I pulled up beside her.

"You forgot something?" she asked, sticking her head inside my passenger side window.

"I'ma take you all the way home so hop in."

She hesitated for a long thirty seconds until she finally reclaimed the seat that she'd vacated a short while ago.

"You hesitating like I'm a serial killer or a serial rapist. You good?" I asked, pulling off from the store.

"I know you ain't no rapist, nigga. I just don't want shit to get awkward if your girl knows that you took me home. If she know like I know, then she a fool for the dick."

"Shut the fuck up with your silly ass!" I replied, laughing heartily.

She laughed too, but we both knew the seriousness in the joke.

"I hear what you saying, and it makes sense because your cousin, Ty, is crazy but don't overthink it. Matter fact, I ain't even gonna take you home. I'ma let you use my other car because you're gonna need mobility to get the job done. You cool with sliding to my other spot and picking it up real quick?" I asked.

"Oh, so now, you wanna take me to your house? I mean, we might as well since we out here."

I grabbed my phone and sent Ty a text before we headed in a different direction, letting her know the plan going forward. With that done, we were back on the move, and half an hour later, we pulled up to my condo's parking lot. I parked a few rows behind my white BMW and just watched everything for a while to see if anything was out of the ordinary.

"Are you paranoid or cautious?" she asked after fifteen minutes of sitting still.

"Both. I ain't been here in a while, so I really don't know what to expect, and I ain't trying to hop out to get shot up."

"Do you wanna go to your condo, or do you just wanna get the car and roll out?" she asked.

"I can think of no justifiable reason to enter my condo alone with you," I said, laughing while being dead ass serious.

"Touché."

"Come on. I'll check out the car, and then, we can leave," I said, stepping out into the bright afternoon sunlight.

I removed the keyless remote from my key ring that I had all my other keys attached to, and then, I pushed the button to unlock the doors. I inspected the interior, looking for anything out of place because I kept all of my cars in pristine condition. I checked under the hood, in the trunk, and then, I committed to my paranoia by actually lying on my back to inspect under the car.

"Everything looks fine so just be careful in my shit because I'm very fond of this car."

"My hero! Thank you for making sure that little ole me will be safe inside of your big, beautiful, white chariot," she gushed, using a passable fake southern accent that made me laugh out loud.

"Safety first, ma'am. Now, I only have to do one more thing, so will you please follow me?" I said, heading back toward my Hellcat.

"Come on, David. I've got shit to do, and you've already wasted an hour playing hide and seek with your damn self."

"Stop pouting and come on," I demanded, taking her by the hand and leading her a little farther away.

I stopped at what I estimated to be a safe distance, turned, and pushed the automatic remote start button for the BMW. Without hesitation or hiccup, the engine came alive, purring dangerously with the 900hp trapped under the hood begging to be set free.

"See, everything is just fine. Now give me the remote so that I can go home and get ready for tonight," she said, holding her hand out impatiently.

"Look, I don't normally let no one drive my shit, so if you get even one scratch on my custom, cocaine white paint job, I'ma fuck up your day. Understand?"

"Boy, shut the fuck up before I key this bitch on video and shoot it to Instagram for you and your girl to watch," she replied seriously.

"Go ahead and play with your life like that. By the way, if you hit one hundred twenty miles per hour, the built-in turbo and nitrous kick in simultaneously, and the speed jumps to one hundred eighty miles per hour before you can blink. Shit will pull your eyelashes off, and all you'll be able to do is hold on."

"David, why the fuck would you have… You know what? I don't wanna know. I won't be driving that fast so thanks for the warning but no thanks. Can I go now?" she asked, clearly out of patience with me.

I moved to hand her the key fob, but something in me hesitated, and then, I realized that I was hearing a strange noise while the car was idling.

"Do you hear that?" I asked, cocking my head to the side to listen better.

"Hear what? Boy, your paranoia has got you all the way spent. Give me the damn…"

While she'd been talking, I'd raised the key fob up and pointed it at the car, and then, I'd tapped the accelerator button that came as a bonus feature for starting/warming the car up. In between one to two RPM, a deafening explosion lifted my beautiful BMW off the ground like it was a fireball made of paper. The pressure from the blast knocked me on my back and had me halfway under my Hellcat. The last thing I saw was Shaomi's little feet leaving the ground like she was a kite catching the breeze. The ringing in my ears was instantaneous, and my thoughts were a jumbled mess, but my body was moving off of instinct and will to survive. Within seconds, I was back on my feet and pulling Shaomi off of the hood of a green Chevy Malibu that was parked one spot over from my Hellcat.

"You okay?" I asked, frantically searching her body to find the source of the blood spreading across her chest.

I found cuts from blown glass, and the back of her head was leaking like someone had turned the water on high. Immediately, I pulled off my shirt and held it to her head, putting her own hand on top of it.

"It's okay. It's gonna be okay. Just hold it there," I said, guiding her toward my Hellcat.

As I got her to the passenger side door, two black Chevy Tahoes came racing into the parking lot and slid to a stop a few feet away from my BMW that was still engulfed in flames. I wanted to believe that the people or person behind the tinted windows of the SUVs were good samaritans, rushing in to save a life, but since they hopped out with guns in their hands, I knew their intentions were bad. In truth, it wasn't so much that they had guns out. It was the obvious modifications to those guns that announced their bad intentions. Cops didn't hop out with drums, extended clips, suppressors, and scopes on their pistols and sub machine guns.

The options of fight or flight were clear, so I pushed Shaomi in the car and ran around the back to hop in the driver's seat, but by the time I reached the gas tank on the driver's side of my car, I saw that the attention of the four men with guns was on us, and they were swiftly moving toward our position. I didn't second guess my hand grabbing my gun or it coming up in front of me right before bullets began to skydive out of the barrel at my insistence. I hit the first two men with three shots apiece in their chests, effectively removing them from the equation. Self-preservation made the other two take cover, but I didn't let that deter me from sending shots in their general direction before I hopped in my car.

"Shoot back," I instructed, tossing my gun in her lap as I slammed the car into gear and stood firm on the gas pedal.

Immediately, my car spun at a forty-five-degree angle, forcing me to pedal the gas so that we could go straight instead of doing donuts. If I tried to exit the parking lot through the traditional exit, that would mean taking my car right past the niggas shooting at me. The moment I saw the tailgate of the Tahoe drop and a 30mm belt fed machine gun appear, I aimed straight for the gates in front of us, embracing the idea of fucking my front end up. That was so much better than the holes from the shit they were shooting.

Chapter 19

"Hang on!" I yelled, ducking low while I floored the gas pedal and rammed through the metal gate.

I heard the wailing cries of the machine gun right before I felt its impact hit the rear driver's side door, pushing the whole car to the right. All I knew in that moment was to keep my foot pressed to the floor because the gun I'd seen sticking out of that Tahoe had the lung capacity to cry for a long while. Once I cleared the gate, I cranked the wheel hard to the right, causing the car to fishtail as we raced away from the madness. In my experience, muthafuckas in suits signified some type of law enforcement in a situation like this, but the ones behind me were moving like real life goons. I had no doubt at this point that whoever they were, they'd blown up my muthafuckin car, and the fact that they were now giving chase let me know that my death was their motivation.

"David, what-what the fuck is going on?" Shaomi asked, still fighting to catch her breath.

"I wish I knew, but I've never seen those dudes."

I could hear the roaring V8 engines gaining on us right before the back window of my Hellcat was reduced to dust by fast flying bullets on a mission. I quickly hung a left, thankful that my car hugged the road this time because it allowed me to put a little more space in between us and death. At first, I had no idea where I was running to, but then, I spotted the freeway on ramp, and I made up my mind. I could still see the SUVs in my rearview mirror as I took the roundabout at seventy miles per hour, but once I reached the straightaway at the bottom of the ramp, I had us moving at one hundred sixty miles per hour, and the black SUVs were just specks in the mirror. There was no way they were catching us now, which allowed my mind to switch over to where we could go. Shaomi was probably safe on her own because I doubted that anybody shooting at me knew who she was, but I couldn't see me gambling with her life.

"Sha Sha, you good? You with me?"

"I'm good. My head is killing me, and I'm seeing triple, but I'm alive I think."

"Okay, listen. I'm not taking you to a hospital, and I don't think it's safe for you to go home. I got a doctor in my apartment building that will check you out if you're good with staying with me," I said.

"Oh, my God, my fucking head hurts! Yeah, I'm good with you. I-I can't go home. We can't bring the danger there... We gotta keep him safe," she moaned.

When I looked over, I saw that the shirt I'd wrapped around her head was completely soaked with blood, and I felt my stomach clutch with fear. I had to get her to a doctor and fast. I set the car to autopilot, which automatically reduced my speed to eighty miles per hour, while I frantically searched for my phone. Once I found it, I immediately called the doctor that I knew stayed on the fifth floor of my building and explained that I had an emergency situation that I needed his help with. I could feel his hesitation come through loud and clear over the phone's line, but as soon as I mentioned money being no object, he was as available as a fulltime hooker during spring break week. I promised to have us there in ten minutes, dropped the phone in my lap so that I could take back control from the autopilot, and then we were back at one hundred sixty miles per hour, weaving through traffic. It was a short eight minutes later when I was helping Shaomi out of the car and into my apartment building. I used the call button in the elevator to contact Dr. Usaf Peleknovich, and he met me as soon as the doors opened on his floor.

"What happened?" he asked in his thick, Russian accent, leading the way while I carried a semi-conscious Shaomi.

"We caught the blow back from a car explosion, and she smacked her head on another car when she landed."

"You two must've been very close because I can smell the explosive on you. Makes me homesick for Mother Russia and the work I grew up doing for the Kremlin. Lay her on the table," he instructed, stepping aside so that I could carry her into the brightly lit dining room.

The layout of his apartment was almost identical to the one I had on the twelfth floor, which meant that he only had two bedrooms, but they were the size of a normal apartment anywhere in the city. Hopefully, he'd converted one to a hospital facility. While I laid her gently on the table, Dr. P. disappeared into one of the bedrooms and came back with his medical bag.

"Are you allergic to any medications, young lady?" he asked.

"N-No, and please give me something strong enough to knock out a horse."

"This I have," he replied, smiling widely as he pulled out a massive syringe and a vial of yellowish liquid.

"Hold her still on her side. The shot will go in her left buttocks," he advised.

I did what he told me, and within a matter of seconds, I could feel her body go limp with relaxation.

"Whew, th-that's good shit," she slurred, closing her eyes with a smile.

"I stitch her head now, and you bring back $20K. Agreed?"

"I'll be right back." I leaned in and whispered in her ear.

I gave the doctor a nod, and then, I left for my own apartment. With each step I took, my anger built so that by the time I walked through my front door, I could see the devil sitting on my brain, laughing his fool head off.

"What happened to you?" Tesha asked, immediately sitting up from her prone position on the couch.

"And where the fuck is your shirt at?" Ty asked, looking up from the baby book she'd been curled up with in the recliner.

I ignored both of their questions and headed straight for my bedroom. My first stop was the safe, where I grabbed enough cash to compensate the doctor. I stuffed the cash in my pocket before grabbing a bulletproof vest from the top shelf and sliding it over my sweaty, bleeding torso. I still had the 9mm on my hip, but it was dirty now, so I tossed it in the safe and pulled out the Sig Sauer p290 .223 carbine with two extra clips. The clips went in my pockets, giving me an extra sixty shots, but I slid the hundred round drum on that bitch to start the party. The Teflon coated, green jacket bullets I was loaded down with could blow through three tanks lined nose to end. By the time I came out of the closet, both Tynesha and Tesha were standing in the doorway, making it clear that I wasn't getting past them without an explanation.

"I don't got time right now so move," I demanded.

"You're a father now, David, so you better fucking make time," Tesha growled in a low, threatening tone.

"Roland had my BMW wired to blow, and it almost got me and Shaomi. She's upstairs getting her head sewed up, so I'ma pay the doctor, and then, I'ma go erase this bitch ass nigga once and for all. Now move," I demanded again.

"You're not mentally ready to go out there right now, David, so just take a minute," Ty said, trying to sound reasonable and rational.

"That's twice that this muthafucka almost killed me, and I'll be goddamned if he gets to take another shot while I just sit back. Cop or no cop, he gotta die. Now move," I growled through clenched teeth.

Both women looked at each other. I didn't know what they saw or communicated, but they suddenly refocused completely on me and took a united step toward me.

"David, please just listen to us," Ty said.

"You can kill him, and we'll help you, just not right this instant," Tesha pleaded.

Even though I knew their intentions were good, I could still feel my impatience causing my rage to rise and redirect toward them. They weren't my enemies, and I knew that, but they were in my way, and I couldn't have that.

"I'ma say it one more time to both of you. Move out..."

"Don't talk to me, David. Talk to your baby," Ty said, lifting her shirt and placing her hand on her smooth, tanned stomach.

Tesha didn't echo her sister's statement verbally, but she lifted her shirt and put her hand on her stomach too. Only her and I knew the significance of her gesture, and the way our eyes locked should've made it transparent to anyone watching us.

"Please, David," Tesha whispered, fighting the tears that I could see welling up in her eyes.

Suddenly, the gun in my hand felt heavy, and I actually began to contemplate putting it down for a second.

"Tynesha? Tesha? Have either of you heard from..."

Tonya's question died before it reached the air once she rounded the corner and saw me.

"David, what did you do?" Tonya asked, sounding both disappointed and heartbroken simultaneously.

"What do you mean?" I asked, feeling the beads of sweat suddenly forming on my forehead.

I hadn't noticed the tablet in Tonya's hand when she'd come in, but she held it up high for me to see. Subconsciously, we all came together, huddled in a circle like bums around an open flame on a cold, northern night. When Tonya pushed the play button for the video frozen on the screen, it got colder in the circle instantly.

"Oh, fuck," Ty murmured.

I watched the fifteen second video clip silently to its conclusion, and then, I hit the button to play it again. The timing of it was the first thing that was obvious in my mind because the clip showed me pull my gun and knock two niggas down with kill shots but not the car explosion before that or their shooting at us afterwards. The quality of the camera was remarkably good on me in my appearance, right down to my tattoos, but it never clearly showed the faces of the men I'd shot. The footage had been sent to Fox News, and they were running with it while calling for my immediate arrest. I mean, they said the words that I was now wanted for murder, but when they listed me as armed and extremely dangerous, we all knew that was police talk meaning shoot to kill.

"Is this real?" Tesha asked, looking at me.

"Yeah, but they're missing the part where my car exploded like a failed middle launch, and four niggas hopped out shooting at me and Shaomi," I replied, frustrated.

"There has to be more footage from another angle then," Ty said.

"No doubt there is but this editing job means that whoever it was has already started the cover up," Tonya said.

Ty's phone suddenly came to life, playing a ring tone from the movie *Black Widow*, which startled us all enough to cause physical reactions. She answered it, and I watched as rising panic took over her features until she was completely submerged under a tsunami of emotion.

"What is it, baby?" I asked, dropping the gun and taking her hand in my own.

For a few moments, all she could do was shake her head like she was attempting to deny all the truth being spoken to her, but emotionally, it became too much, and she just disconnected the call.

"Tynesha? What is it, baby?" Tonya asked, visibly concerned.

"That was-that was Carrie, my girl that works for the law firm who got David out for me. She said... she told me that Roland is dead, and the cops just identified his body."

"Okay, so that's a reason to celebrate, bitch!" Tesha said excitedly.

I could tell by the look in Ty's eyes that there was more to the story though.

"Why aren't you excited, sweetheart?" I asked, squeezing her hand in mine as fear gripped my heart.

I'd really believed her when she'd said the baby was mine, but her reaction to his death could mean there was a deep seeded reason she was mourning his passing.

"The bullets they pulled out of Roland match other bullets from the shooting in your condo parking lot... and they're saying that you fired those bullets," Ty replied.

"That would only be possible if Roland was one of the men that jumped out. So, was he one of the shooters?" Tesha asked.

"No, I don't-I don't know. It all happened so fast, and I was just trying not to let me or Shaomi get hit," I replied, trying to see it in slow motion in my mind so that I could see everything.

"There's more though," Ty said ominously, looking from me to her sister.

For a split second, I thought she knew about me fucking Tesha somehow, but I quickly realized that if that was the case, then somebody would be dead already.

"Roland's death led to a search of his house apparently, for God knows what, and they found another gun there that wasn't his. This particular gun was tied to an unsolved homicide that was high profile a while back... and Tesha's prints are supposedly on the gun," Ty said.

"Son of a bitch," I said, shaking my head as disbelief gave way to feelings of extreme anxiety.

"Tesha..." Tonya said, resting her hand on her daughter's shoulder.

"It's-it's okay. I can beat this," Tesha said hollowly.

"What did Carrie say about her firm defending us?" I asked, hopeful to have legal minds at work already.

"That's the worst part, bae! Her firm can't represent you or Tesha... because they're in bed with Zoe Pound," Ty replied, her voice cracking with desperation.

"What the fuck does that have to do with anything?" Tonya asked heatedly.

Truth hit me like a lightning bolt, illuminating my mind in a way that made the facts glow like neon lights impossible to ignore. There was no such thing as a coincidence, and when I accepted that, then today's actions made more sense. Zoe Pound was cutting their loses and eliminating the threats, which meant that eventually, all of us involved had to die.

"They're coming for us," I said calmly.

"And they're using the law and law enforcement to make it a legal execution," Ty surmised.

"We can't let that shit happen! We gotta do whatever to keep our family safe," Tonya said.

"Protect the family," Tesha said, putting her hand on Ty's stomach.

Ty reached out and put her hand on Tesha's stomach.

"Protect the family," Ty said, looking lovingly at me.

Tonya grabbed both of her daughter's free hands and placed them on her own stomach, and the look she gave me caused my heart to flutter with shades of panic.

"We protect the family. Right, David?" Tonya asked.

All eyes swung my way, but my focus remained on Tonya. The longer we stated at each other, the more convinced I became that Tonya wasn't too old to have a lethal secret.

"We always protect the family... After all, family only means one thing," I replied.

"And what's that?" Tynesha asked curiously.

I looked each woman in the eyes before I spoke again.

"For All Mine, I'll Lay Yours... F-a-m-i-l-y."

To be continued...

Lock Down Publications and Ca$h Presents
Assisted Publishing Packages

BASIC PACKAGE $499 Editing Cover Design Formatting	UPGRADED PACKAGE $800 Typing Editing Cover Design Formatting
ADVANCE PACKAGE $1,200 Typing Editing Cover Design Formatting Copyright registration Proofreading Upload book to Amazon	LDP SUPREME PACKAGE $1,500 Typing Editing Cover Design Formatting Copyright registration Proofreading Set up Amazon account Upload book to Amazon Advertise on LDP, Amazon and Facebook Page

***Other services available upon request.
Additional charges may apply

Lock Down Publications
P.O. Box 944
Stockbridge, GA 30281-9998
Phone: 470 303-9761

Submission Guideline

Submit the first three chapters of your completed manuscript to ldpsubmissions@gmail.com. In the subject line add **Your Book's Title**. The manuscript must be in a Word Doc file and sent as an attachment. Document should be in Times New Roman, double spaced, and in size 12 font. Also, provide your synopsis and full contact information. If sending multiple submissions, they must each be in a separate email.

Have a story but no way to send it electronically? You can still submit to LDP/Ca$h Presents. Send in the first three chapters, written or typed, of your completed manuscript to:

LDP: Submissions Dept
P.O. Box 944
Stockbridge, GA 30281-9998

DO NOT send original manuscript. Must be a duplicate.
Provide your synopsis and a cover letter containing your full contact information.

Thanks for considering LDP and Ca$h Presents.

NEW RELEASES

BLOODLINE OF A SAVAGE **BY PRINCE A. TAUHID**

THE MURDER QUEENS 4 **BY MICHAEL GALLON**

THE BUTTERFLY MAFIA **BY FUMIYA PAYNE**

KING KILLA 2 **BY VINCENT "VITTO" HOLLOWAY**

BABY, I'M WINTERTIME COLD 3 **BY MEESHA**

THESE VICIOUS STREETS **BY PRINCE A. TAUHID**

TIL DEATH 2 **BY ARYANNA**

CITY OF SMOKE 2 **BY MOLOTTI**

STEPPERS **BY KING RIO**

THE LANE **BY KEN-KEN SPENCE**

MONEY GAME 2 **BY SMOOVE DOLLA**

THE BLACK DIAMOND CARTEL **BY SAYNOMORE**

CRIME BOSS 2 **BY PLAYA RAY**

THUG OF SPADES **BY COREY ROBINSON**

LOVE IN THE TRENCHES 2 **BY COREY ROBINSON**

TIL DEATH 3 **BY ARYANNA**

THE BIRTH OF A GANGSTER 4 **BY DELMONT PLAYER**

PRODUCT OF THE STREETS **BY DEMOND "MONEY" ANDERSON**

Coming Soon from Lock Down Publications/Ca$h Presents

BLOOD OF A BOSS VI
SHADOWS OF THE GAME II
TRAP BASTARD II
By **Askari**

LOYAL TO THE GAME IV
By **T.J. & Jelissa**

TRUE SAVAGE VIII
MIDNIGHT CARTEL IV
DOPE BOY MAGIC IV
CITY OF KINGZ III
NIGHTMARE ON SILENT AVE II
THE PLUG OF LIL MEXICO II
CLASSIC CITY II
By **Chris Green**

BLAST FOR ME III
A SAVAGE DOPEBOY III
CUTTHROAT MAFIA III
DUFFLE BAG CARTEL VII
HEARTLESS GOON VI
By **Ghost**

A HUSTLER'S DECEIT III
KILL ZONE II
BAE BELONGS TO ME III
TIL DEATH II
By **Aryanna**

KING OF THE TRAP III
By **T.J. Edwards**

GORILLAZ IN THE BAY V
3X KRAZY III
STRAIGHT BEAST MODE III
By **De'Kari**

KINGPIN KILLAZ IV
STREET KINGS III
PAID IN BLOOD III
CARTEL KILLAZ IV
DOPE GODS III
By **Hood Rich**

SINS OF A HUSTLA II
By **ASAD**

YAYO V
BRED IN THE GAME 2
By **S. Allen**

THE STREETS WILL TALK II
By **Yolanda Moore**

SON OF A DOPE FIEND III
HEAVEN GOT A GHETTO III
SKI MASK MONEY III
By **Renta**

LOYALTY AIN'T PROMISED III
By **Keith Williams**

I'M NOTHING WITHOUT HIS LOVE II
SINS OF A THUG II
TO THE THUG I LOVED BEFORE II
IN A HUSTLER I TRUST II
By **Monet Dragun**

QUIET MONEY IV
EXTENDED CLIP III
THUG LIFE IV
By **Trai'Quan**

THE STREETS MADE ME IV
By **Larry D. Wright**

IF YOU CROSS ME ONCE III
ANGEL V
By **Anthony Fields**

THE STREETS WILL NEVER CLOSE IV
By **K'ajji**

HARD AND RUTHLESS III
KILLA KOUNTY IV
By **Khufu**

MONEY GAME III
By **Smoove Dolla**

MURDA WAS THE CASE III
Elijah R. Freeman

AN UNFORESEEN LOVE IV
BABY, I'M WINTERTIME COLD III
By **Meesha**

QUEEN OF THE ZOO III
By **Black Migo**

CONFESSIONS OF A JACKBOY III
By **Nicholas Lock**

JACK BOYS VS DOPE BOYS IV
A GANGSTA'S QUR'AN V
COKE GIRLZ II
COKE BOYS II
LIFE OF A SAVAGE V
CHI'RAQ GANGSTAS V
SOSA GANG III
BRONX SAVAGES II
BODYMORE KINGPINS II
By **Romell Tukes**

KING KILLA II
By **Vincent "Vitto" Holloway**

BETRAYAL OF A THUG III
By **Fre$h**

THE MURDER QUEENS III
By **Michael Gallon**

THE BIRTH OF A GANGSTER III
By **Delmont Player**

TREAL LOVE II
By **Le'Monica Jackson**

FOR THE LOVE OF BLOOD III
By **Jamel Mitchell**

RAN OFF ON DA PLUG II
By **Paper Boi Rari**

HOOD CONSIGLIERE III
By **Keese**

PRETTY GIRLS DO NASTY THINGS II
By **Nicole Goosby**

PROTÉGÉ OF A LEGEND III
LOVE IN THE TRENCHES II
By **Corey Robinson**

IT'S JUST ME AND YOU II
By **Ah'Million**

FOREVER GANGSTA III
By **Adrian Dulan**

GORILLAZ IN THE TRENCHES II
By **SayNoMore**

THE COCAINE PRINCESS VIII
By **King Rio**

CRIME BOSS II
By **Playa Ray**

LOYALTY IS EVERYTHING III
By **Molotti**

HERE TODAY GONE TOMORROW II
By **Fly Rock**

REAL G'S MOVE IN SILENCE II
By **Von Diesel**

GRIMEY WAYS IV
By **Ray Vinci**

Available Now

RESTRAINING ORDER I & II
By **CA$H & Coffee**

LOVE KNOWS NO BOUNDARIES I II & III
By **Coffee**

RAISED AS A GOON I, II, III & IV
BRED BY THE SLUMS I, II, III
BLAST FOR ME I & II
ROTTEN TO THE CORE I II III
A BRONX TALE I, II, III
DUFFLE BAG CARTEL I II III IV V VI
HEARTLESS GOON I II III IV V
A SAVAGE DOPEBOY I II
DRUG LORDS I II III
CUTTHROAT MAFIA I II
KING OF THE TRENCHES
By **Ghost**

LAY IT DOWN I & II
LAST OF A DYING BREED I II
BLOOD STAINS OF A SHOTTA I & II III
By **Jamaica**

LOYAL TO THE GAME I II III
LIFE OF SIN I, II III
By **TJ & Jelissa**

IF LOVING HIM IS WRONG…I & II
LOVE ME EVEN WHEN IT HURTS I II III
By **Jelissa**

175

IMMA DIE BOUT MINE | BY ARYANNA

BLOODY COMMAS I & II
SKI MASK CARTEL I, II & III
KING OF NEW YORK I II, III IV V
RISE TO POWER I II III
COKE KINGS I II III IV V
BORN HEARTLESS I II III IV
KING OF THE TRAP I II
By **T.J. Edwards**

WHEN THE STREETS CLAP BACK I & II III
THE HEART OF A SAVAGE I II III IV
MONEY MAFIA I II
LOYAL TO THE SOIL I II III
By **Jibril Williams**

A DISTINGUISHED THUG STOLE MY HEART I II &
III
LOVE SHOULDN'T HURT I II III IV
RENEGADE BOYS I II III IV
PAID IN KARMA I II III
SAVAGE STORMS I II III
AN UNFORESEEN LOVE I II III
BABY, I'M WINTERTIME COLD I II
By **Meesha**

A GANGSTER'S CODE I &, II III
A GANGSTER'S SYN I II III
THE SAVAGE LIFE I II III
CHAINED TO THE STREETS I II III
BLOOD ON THE MONEY I II III
A GANGSTA'S PAIN I II III
By **J-Blunt**

PUSH IT TO THE LIMIT
By **Bre' Hayes**

BLOOD OF A BOSS I, II, III, IV, V
SHADOWS OF THE GAME
TRAP BASTARD
By **Askari**

THE STREETS BLEED MURDER I, II & III
THE HEART OF A GANGSTA I II& III
By **Jerry Jackson**

CUM FOR ME I II III IV V VI VII VIII
An **LDP Erotica Collaboration**

BRIDE OF A HUSTLA I II & II
THE FETTI GIRLS I, II& III
CORRUPTED BY A GANGSTA I, II III, IV
BLINDED BY HIS LOVE
THE PRICE YOU PAY FOR LOVE I, II ,III
DOPE GIRL MAGIC I II III
By **Destiny Skai**

WHEN A GOOD GIRL GOES BAD
By **Adrienne**

A GANGSTER'S REVENGE I II III & IV
THE BOSS MAN'S DAUGHTERS I II III IV V
A SAVAGE LOVE I & II
BAE BELONGS TO ME I II
A HUSTLER'S DECEIT I, II, III
WHAT BAD BITCHES DO I, II, III
SOUL OF A MONSTER I II III
KILL ZONE
A DOPE BOY'S QUEEN I II III
TIL DEATH
By **Aryanna**

THE COST OF LOYALTY I II III
By Kweli

A KINGPIN'S AMBITION
A KINGPIN'S AMBITION **II**
I MURDER FOR THE DOUGH
By **Ambitious**

TRUE SAVAGE I II III IV V VI VII
DOPE BOY MAGIC I, II, III
MIDNIGHT CARTEL I II III
CITY OF KINGZ I II
NIGHTMARE ON SILENT AVE
THE PLUG OF LIL MEXICO II
CLASSIC CITY
By **Chris Green**

A DOPEBOY'S PRAYER
By **Eddie "Wolf" Lee**

THE KING CARTEL I, II & III
By **Frank Gresham**

THESE NIGGAS AIN'T LOYAL I, II & III
By **Nikki Tee**

GANGSTA SHYT I II &III
By **CATO**

THE ULTIMATE BETRAYAL
By **Phoenix**

BOSS'N UP I, II & III
By **Royal Nicole**

IMMA DIE BOUT MINE | BY ARYANNA

I LOVE YOU TO DEATH
By **Destiny J**

I RIDE FOR MY HITTA
I STILL RIDE FOR MY HITTA
By **Misty Holt**

LOVE & CHASIN' PAPER
By **Qay Crockett**

TO DIE IN VAIN
SINS OF A HUSTLA
By **ASAD**

BROOKLYN HUSTLAZ
By **Boogsy Morina**

BROOKLYN ON LOCK I & II
By **Sonovia**

GANGSTA CITY
By **Teddy Duke**

A DRUG KING AND HIS DIAMOND I & II III
A DOPEMAN'S RICHES
HER MAN, MINE'S TOO I, II
CASH MONEY HO'S
THE WIFEY I USED TO BE I II
PRETTY GIRLS DO NASTY THINGS
By Nicole Goosby

LIPSTICK KILLAH I, II, III
CRIME OF PASSION I II & III
FRIEND OR FOE I II III
By **Mimi**

TRAPHOUSE KING I II & III
KINGPIN KILLAZ I II III
STREET KINGS I II
PAID IN BLOOD I II
CARTEL KILLAZ I II III
DOPE GODS I II
By **Hood Rich**

STEADY MOBBN' I, II, III
THE STREETS STAINED MY SOUL I II III
By **Marcellus Allen**

WHO SHOT YA I, II, III
SON OF A DOPE FIEND I II
HEAVEN GOT A GHETTO I II
SKI MASK MONEY I II
By **Renta**

GORILLAZ IN THE BAY I II III IV
TEARS OF A GANGSTA I II
3X KRAZY I II
STRAIGHT BEAST MODE I II
By **DE'KARI**

TRIGGADALE I II III
MURDA WAS THE CASE I II
By **Elijah R. Freeman**

THE STREETS ARE CALLING
By **Duquie Wilson**

SLAUGHTER GANG I II III
RUTHLESS HEART I II III
By **Willie Slaughter**

IMMA DIE BOUT MINE | BY ARYANNA

GOD BLESS THE TRAPPERS I, II, III
THESE SCANDALOUS STREETS I, II, III
FEAR MY GANGSTA I, II, III IV, V
THESE STREETS DON'T LOVE NOBODY I, II
BURY ME A G I, II, III, IV, V
A GANGSTA'S EMPIRE I, II, III, IV
THE DOPEMAN'S BODYGAURD I II
THE REALEST KILLAZ I II III
THE LAST OF THE OGS I II III
By **Tranay Adams**

MARRIED TO A BOSS I II III
By **Destiny Skai & Chris Green**

KINGZ OF THE GAME I II III IV V VI VII
CRIME BOSS
By **Playa Ray**

FUK SHYT
By **Blakk Diamond**

DON'T F#CK WITH MY HEART I II
By **Linnea**

ADDICTED TO THE DRAMA I II III
IN THE ARM OF HIS BOSS II
By **Jamila**

YAYO I II III IV
A SHOOTER'S AMBITION I II
BRED IN THE GAME
By **S. Allen**

LOYALTY AIN'T PROMISED I II
By **Keith Williams**

TRAP GOD I II III
RICH $AVAGE I II III
MONEY IN THE GRAVE I II III
By **Martell Troublesome Bolden**

FOREVER GANGSTA I II
GLOCKS ON SATIN SHEETS I II
By **Adrian Dulan**

TOE TAGZ I II III IV
LEVELS TO THIS SHYT I II
IT'S JUST ME AND YOU
By **Ah'Million**

KINGPIN DREAMS I II III
RAN OFF ON DA PLUG
By **Paper Boi Rari**

CONFESSIONS OF A GANGSTA I II III IV
CONFESSIONS OF A JACKBOY I II
By **Nicholas Lock**

I'M NOTHING WITHOUT HIS LOVE
SINS OF A THUG
TO THE THUG I LOVED BEFORE
A GANGSTA SAVED XMAS
IN A HUSTLER I TRUST
By **Monet Dragun**

QUIET MONEY I II III
THUG LIFE I II III
EXTENDED CLIP I II
A GANGSTA'S PARADISE
By **Trai'Quan**

IMMA DIE BOUT MINE | BY ARYANNA

CAUGHT UP IN THE LIFE I II III
THE STREETS NEVER LET GO I II III
By **Robert Baptiste**

NEW TO THE GAME I II III
MONEY, MURDER & MEMORIES I II III
By **Malik D. Rice**

CREAM I II III
THE STREETS WILL TALK
By **Yolanda Moore**

LIFE OF A SAVAGE I II III IV
A GANGSTA'S QUR'AN I II III IV
MURDA SEASON I II III
GANGLAND CARTEL I II III
CHI'RAQ GANGSTAS I II III IV
KILLERS ON ELM STREET I II III
JACK BOYZ N DA BRONX I II III
A DOPEBOY'S DREAM I II III
JACK BOYS VS DOPE BOYS I II III
COKE GIRLZ
COKE BOYS
SOSA GANG I II
BRONX SAVAGES
BODYMORE KINGPINS
By **Romell Tukes**

THE STREETS MADE ME I II III
By **Larry D. Wright**

CONCRETE KILLA I II III
VICIOUS LOYALTY I II III
By **Kingpen**

IMMA DIE BOUT MINE | BY ARYANNA

THE ULTIMATE SACRIFICE I, II, III, IV, V, VI
KHADIFI
IF YOU CROSS ME ONCE I II
ANGEL I II III IV
IN THE BLINK OF AN EYE
By **Anthony Fields**

THE LIFE OF A HOOD STAR
By **Ca$h & Rashia Wilson**

THE STREETS WILL NEVER CLOSE I II III
By **K'ajji**

NIGHTMARES OF A HUSTLA I II III
By **King Dream**

HARD AND RUTHLESS I II
MOB TOWN 251
THE BILLIONAIRE BENTLEYS I II III
REAL G'S MOVE IN SILENCE
By **Von Diesel**

GHOST MOB
By **Stilloan Robinson**

MOB TIES I II III IV V VI
SOUL OF A HUSTLER, HEART OF A KILLER I II
GORILLAZ IN THE TRENCHES
By **SayNoMore**

BODYMORE MURDERLAND I II III
THE BIRTH OF A GANGSTER I II
By **Delmont Player**

IMMA DIE BOUT MINE | BY ARYANNA

FOR THE LOVE OF A BOSS
By **C. D. Blue**

KILLA KOUNTY I II III IV
By Khufu

MOBBED UP I II III IV
THE BRICK MAN I II III IV V
THE COCAINE PRINCESS I II III IV V VI VII
By **King Rio**

MONEY GAME I II
By **Smoove Dolla**

A GANGSTA'S KARMA I II III
By **FLAME**

KING OF THE TRENCHES I II III
By **GHOST & TRANAY ADAMS**

QUEEN OF THE ZOO I II
By **Black Migo**

GRIMEY WAYS I II III
By **Ray Vinci**

XMAS WITH AN ATL SHOOTER
By **Ca$h & Destiny Skai**

KING KILLA
By **Vincent "Vitto" Holloway**

BETRAYAL OF A THUG I II
By **Fre$h**

IMMA DIE BOUT MINE | BY ARYANNA

THE MURDER QUEENS I II
By **Michael Gallon**

TREAL LOVE
By **Le'Monica Jackson**

FOR THE LOVE OF BLOOD I II
By **Jamel Mitchell**

HOOD CONSIGLIERE I II
By **Keese**

PROTÉGÉ OF A LEGEND I II
LOVE IN THE TRENCHES
By **Corey Robinson**

BORN IN THE GRAVE I II III
By **Self Made Tay**

MOAN IN MY MOUTH
By **XTASY**

TORN BETWEEN A GANGSTER AND A
GENTLEMAN
By **J-BLUNT & Miss Kim**

LOYALTY IS EVERYTHING I II
By **Molotti**

HERE TODAY GONE TOMORROW
By **Fly Rock**

PILLOW PRINCESS
By **S. Hawkins**

IMMA DIE BOUT MINE | BY ARYANNA

SANCTIFIED AND HORNY
by **XTASY**

THE PLUG OF LIL MEXICO 2
by **CHRIS GREEN**

THE BLACK DIAMOND CARTEL
by **SAYNOMORE**

THE BIRTH OF A GANGSTER 3
by **DELMONT PLAYER**

BOOKS BY LDP'S CEO, CA$H

TRUST IN NO MAN
TRUST IN NO MAN 2
TRUST IN NO MAN 3
BONDED BY BLOOD
SHORTY GOT A THUG
THUGS CRY
THUGS CRY 2
THUGS CRY 3
TRUST NO BITCH
TRUST NO BITCH 2
TRUST NO BITCH 3
TIL MY CASKET DROPS
RESTRAINING ORDER
RESTRAINING ORDER 2
IN LOVE WITH A CONVICT
LIFE OF A HOOD STAR
XMAS WITH AN ATL SHOOTER

www.ingramcontent.com/pod-product-compliance
Lightning Source LLC
Chambersburg PA
CBHW070517260626
47161CB00004B/1578